LAST CALL

By

PHYLLIS

SMALLMAN

Praise For The Sherri Travis Series

The Sherri Travis series was listed as one of the top 6 mystery series for 2010 summer reads by Good Morning America --World News.com.

"The Sherri Travis Mysteries started out well and have gotten better . . . The writing keeps getting tighter, and Smallman knows how to crank up the reader's tension . . . One can't help wanting more and anticipating the next book in this entertaining and fast- paced series." — *National Post*

"A series that gives the reader a casual style and storytelling with staying power." — *Hamilton Spectator*

"Florida has never seemed so appealing and appalling as it does in the Sherri Travis novels." —*Toronto Star*

"In Sherri Travis, [Smallman] has created a sassy, plucky heroine who isn't afraid to get her hands dirty and ask the questions that need to be asked." —*Cozy Mystery Book Review*

Also by Phyllis Smallman

Copyright © 2017 Phyllis Smallman

Phyllis Smallman Publishing

www.phyllissmallman.com

Published in both Print and
Electronic Formats

Print ISBN   9780992053697

Electronic ISBN   9780992053680

Smallman, Phyllis, author
Last Call / Phyllis Smallman.

(A Sherri Travis Mystery ; 7)

Acknowledgements

Thank you to my writer friends who read my rough manuscript and improved it: Elaine Kozak and Kristina Stanley. You were so very generous with your time and comments.

I would also like to thank my editor, Linda Pearce, for her attention to detail. She can be reached at pearce@ucalgary.ca

For Lee

— Always and ever —

Chapter 1

Lunging into water up to my knees, I threw myself into the canoe, tipping it wildly until it threatened to roll. The paddle cracked against the side, signaling where I was. A yell went up in the dark, "She's here!"

Beside me, Marley screamed, "Slow down."

I gulped air. The terrifying memory of the Everglades receded and the sun shone again, but my heart still hammered in my ears and fear still trickled sweat down my body.

"Shit, Sherri, you're going to kill us. Pay attention!"

"I am," I said, but she knew it wasn't true. Terrifying images, dangerous waking nightmares, were a daily part of my life since Clay's murder. I glanced over at Marley. She had her bare feet braced against the dash, one hand locked to the back of my seat and the other one clutching the door, ready for the crash. The freckles she hated stood out on her pale face. Trying to make light of her fears, and diminish any fault of mine, I waved at the empty road in front of us where only a mirage of heat danced on the fiery asphalt. "There's no one but us out here. What are you afraid of?"

"Dying, you idiot."

The speedometer was closer to one hundred than it was to ninety. I backed off a little and took a deep breath. All the crosses and plastic flowers along the road said she might have a point.

"Pull over," she said. "I'll drive." I eased up a little more on the gas but I didn't pull over.

We'd come down the west coast of Florida from Cypress Island, and now we were going east on Alligator Alley toward Miami. "You drove to Fort Myers so I drive the rest of the way. That was the deal," I said. Ahead of us, a flamingo flew low over the road, racing us toward the Atlantic. "Relax and enjoy the scenery." I needed to be in control. I was the only one who could deal with the disaster when it came, and my head was in a place where the only thing coming was disaster.

The Everglades, mostly flat grasslands, looked peaceful and benign as they flashed by the car window, but I knew all about the alligators, boa constrictors and psychopaths waiting out there, knew it only takes one small mistake, like the one I made, to change your life forever. The night my pickup was hijacked, and I was left alone in the Everglades, all the violence that followed was because I hadn't been paying attention. I know now that life and death can depend on small things. I watch for those things, try and keep control of the situation so I stay safe. Well, at least that's what I tell myself I'm doing.

Shaking her head Marley said, "You really gotta get a grip, Sherri. Lexi is counting on you. You can't let her down." She raised her hands, palms out, as though she was bestowing a blessing. "Don't look back. It's over." It wasn't true. For me it would never be over. "Let it go," she added.

Normally, Marley wants everything laid out – beats that dead horse until her arm falls off. Not this time. For Marley, Clay's murder was something to bury and forget.

"I just want you to…" I started but she interrupted with, "I know. And I do understand." Her voice was loud and angry. "I should. You've told me enough times." She turned away from me to stare out the window.

Marley didn't know shit about what I was feeling… didn't know that when I closed my eyes I saw the astonishment on Clay's face, surprise that was quickly replaced by incredible sadness at the knowledge that he was dying.

I fought for coolness, kept my voice level. "Being in the Everglades again…well, it brings it all back."

Her hands flew up to her head and buried themselves in her short red curls as if she truly intended to tear her hair out. "Brings it back? As if it ever went away." She took a big gulp of air, fighting to be calm. "Tell you what. For the next two days, let's not talk about the past. No reality until we head north again. Agreed?"

"Sure." Even to my ear the word lacked conviction.

3

She twisted on the seat to face me. "You think you can go two days without talking about money, work, or Clay's murder?"

"No problem." She snorted in disbelief. "Let's put a little money on it. Every time either of us talks about real life, we pay the other five bucks."

I nodded. "Prepare to lose your money, honey."

"Hah! You can't do it." She was probably right. Lockjaw was my only chance of staving off bankruptcy.

We left the Everglades behind, past Homestead heading for the Keys. Marley reached out and played with the radio dial. "How much trouble is Lexi in?" The dial swung to a news bulletin from the National Hurricane Center in Florida. The statement informed us that a tropical disturbance, south of the Bahamas, was becoming better organized and forming into a circular shape and now it had been given a name. The first named storm of the season, it was being called Alma. With the Gulf stream three degrees hotter than normal there was a very high probability of it turning into a hurricane. Residents of Florida were advised to listen to their news channels for further bulletins.

You couldn't tell there was any danger from the weather by looking out the window. It was a perfect Florida day, in the nineties with high cumulus clouds and light winds, but when we crossed a short bridge the foam-capped waves, racing ahead of the storm, were higher than normal.

"Shit," Marley said. "Key West is no place to be in a big gale."

"We'll be gone long before it hits. Don't worry about it."

"If I didn't worry, my brain wouldn't see any action at all."

I laughed and for a moment the tension between us eased.

She said, "Seriously, with all those little causeways, how do they evacuate the Keys in a storm?"

"Slowly, very slowly."

Highway one, the only road to Key West, is a two-lane highway running down to the tip of Florida. The road is built on a string of small outcrops of land called keys. Bridges and causeways connect these keys, Sugarloaf Key, Indian Key, Islamorada and Key Largo, bits of land so small that sometimes it feels as if you're driving on water when you're crossing them. With the Gulf of Mexico on the right and the Straits of Florida on the left, you rise over turquoise water like a bird flying into a painting of Paradise, hang suspended between heaven and earth, and then swoop down onto a green hummock of land before rising again. My spirits lifted with each mad dash into the sky, but Marley was right. The two-lane road is the Main Street of all the small towns along the way. In an evacuation, the roads would be clogged. It would be hell getting out ahead of a serious storm.

"Let's just make sure we're gone before there's a problem," she said and switched the dial to Conch Country at

5

98.7 FM. "This country music will get you in the mood for the Rawhide Saloon."

"Oh, I'm ready." It was true. Normally by this time of the day I'd have a nice buzz going and sustain it until closing time, when the real job got done. "But we don't need all those hurtin' songs — songs of leaving home, missing home or wanting to go home. We don't want to hear anything about home. Find something else."

So, with Taylor Swift exhorting us to shake it off, we headed down to Key West for a little fun. Even with that thought, a cloud passed in front of the sun.

Chapter 2

The thing I love most about Key West is that the bars are like mental wards with music and a happy hour.

"Hee haw," I shouted as I pulled up in front of the Rawhide Saloon. I'd spent a lot of time in Key West, but this was my first time at the Rawhide. I could see right off it was my kind of place. A long narrow building, constructed from raw wood, it could have been stolen from a western on AMC. On the roof a red neon cowboy danced, trying to lasso a moon that blinked, *Drinks*. A porch ran along the front. Smokers, and diners waiting for a table, sat on bare wooden benches with their feet up on the railing. The party was already happening out here, but when we walked through the door my heart started beating faster. Let the fun begin.

Lexi Divine, the manager of the Rawhide, met us at the door with her arms spread wide to embrace us. "Welcome to Key West."

After a bone breaking hug, she pushed me away and studied me while I did the same to her. Everything about Lexi was perfect. Glamorous and feminine, she made even those of us born female feel inadequate, but around her eyes were small lines of worry that hadn't been there when I'd seen her six months earlier.

Lexi doesn't dress like the rest of us. She puts on a costume. That night she was playing Marilyn Monroe to a packed house. Dressed in white, her favorite color, her halter dress fit tightly to just above the knees and then flared out in a twelve-inch flounce. Lexi had been born Mason Cartwright junior, a name she gave back to her father the night he threw her out of his house and told her she was dead to her family. That night, Mason Cartwright became Lexi Divine. "How was your trip?" she asked.

"It took us two hours to go the last fifty miles." I was searching the crowd for a waiter as I spoke. "It left me real thirsty."

"Now that's a problem I can solve." Lexi took my arm and led the way to a reserved table, saying, "I hope you can solve mine just as easily, Sherri."

I wasn't really thinking about her worries. I just wanted to dive into a bottle and forget my own.

The three of us — Marley Hemming, Lexi Divine and me, Sherri Travis — sat in a red leather booth halfway down the room on the left. The premiere table, it was raised a foot above the rest giving us an uninterrupted view of the action. The Rawhide boasts that it has the longest bar in Florida. I don't know if that's true or not, but from my extensive investigation of bars I'd say they had a shot at the title. This one ran the length of the room on the far wall, probably thirty feet long, while on the left was a series of raised booths in red leather. A small stage at the far end of the room was raised about three feet above a tiny dance floor. Hardened by booze and polished by thousands of dancers, it overflowed with gyrating bodies. In between the stage and entrance was pure craziness.

This seemed to be a particularly weird night even for Key West. While it was too early for the real characters to come out to play, the Rawhide already pulsed with too loud music over screams of laughter and a mood that trembled on the edge of crazed. The room was a swirling kaleidoscope of waiters — disguised as cowboys, hookers — pretending to be models, together with wide eyed sightseers fresh off a cruise liner and pretending to fit in. I bet those tourists, who had to be back on their ship by midnight and were making the most of their Cinderella stop, were already trying to decide how they were going to describe this madhouse when they got back to Omaha. But how do you explain the freak acts in a sideshow where everyone has lost their mind? For me it felt like a haven. I took a deep breath of perfume, booze and pheromones, and I smiled.

We barely had a drink in our hands before Lexi started to tell us about her problem. "The owner thinks I'm dipping into the take and if I don't find out who's actually doing it I'm going to be thrown out on my cute little butt. This is the best job I ever had. I don't want to lose it — or to leave Key West."

"Who would want to leave Key West?" I held my arms out wide. "This is a swell town." A hundred and sixty miles from Miami but only ninety from Cuba, Key West is a million miles from reality and that's just where I wanted to be. "I've never seen so many bars in one place."

Lexi frowned. "That was the problem when we opened the Rawhide — too many bars. Country was the only theme that wasn't taken."

"Well, Yippee-Ki-Yay, I say. A great idea. All those…" My hands described circles before pointing to the bare-bottomed waiters who were wearing chaps and little else. "Lovely."

"It won't be lovely if I get fired. I won't find another job in this town. That's the thing about a small town, your reputation is everything." She leaned toward me, worried and intense. "You have to help me, Sherri."

"Well, give me a minute. I only just drove over the causeway." I picked up my nearly empty wine glass and waggled it back and forth in front of her. Nothing subtle about me.

Lexi took the hint and raised a hand to a passing waiter and then leaned closer so she could be heard over the noise. "I know I'm losing a couple of hundred a night but I can't figure out how."

"Have you checked your inventory? Made sure no one is selling food or booze out the back door?"

"Double checked and it all seems to balance. The food sales tally with inventory. The bar staff have to sign for every bottle they take out of stock and I check what's on the bar at the start of every day."

"It will be the bar. When you deal with cash and a high number of transactions there's lots of room to skim." It was unlikely I'd catch anything, but I promised myself I'd stay sober and watch — sort of pace myself. Even as I made that commitment, I raised my glass.

Marley was totally uninterested in the problems of running a bar. She dipped a chip into the salsa, pointed it at Lexi, and asked, "So, can you still pee standing up?"

I knew Lexi better than Marley did. I watched Lexi's dazzling surface, only too aware of the dangerous underside to her beauty. I'd known Lexi most of my life and she'd always had a deep well of anger that could overflow at the tiniest provocation. I held my breath and waited. Some small rudeness or perceived disrespect would have her exploding into loud and embarrassing recrimination. Lexi always won these contests because no one else could stand the mortification of her attacks. Winning added to Lexi's sense of entitlement, her belief in her own rightness. This demanding side of her character was balanced by an incredible sense of fun and an outrageous sense of humor. I hadn't seen either of these since we'd arrived. The Lexi Marley and I'd found on arriving in Key West was one who was worried and preoccupied.

Lexi arched an elegant eyebrow at me.

"Don't look at me." I reached for my glass, protecting the booze at all costs. "Marley is flying solo here."

Lexi smiled but there were warning lights flashing in her eyes. Even on a good day you don't want to annoy her and this certainly wasn't one of those. I eased away from Marley. If anything was going to be thrown, I wasn't going to be in the line of fire.

Lexi studied her polish for a heartbeat and then she sat even straighter, shoulders back and chest out. "Yes, I still have all the appendages I was born with."

I relaxed a little. But fear of stepping in caca has never stopped Marley. "But I don't get it." She started ticking off a list on her fingers. "You've had breast implants, you're taking estrogen, had your butt remodeled and electrolysis …why not go the whole nine yards and have those extra bits and pieces cut off?"

I set down my glass. "Excuse me." Not even free booze could keep me there while Lexi explained why she was still fishing with the same old tackle. I slid to the edge of the booth to make a hasty exit before the blood started flowing.

Marley looked at me in confusion. "Where are you going?"

"This conversation is making me blush."

Marley's eyebrows rose in mock astonishment. "I didn't know you could."

"I just don't like girl-talk of a medical nature." I was already on my feet and standing by the table. A roar went up from the crowd. We turned to the stage.

One of the features of the Rawhide Saloon is the delicious waiters. They wear leather chaps, designed to leave most of their derrieres exposed, and tiny little vests with lots of leather fringe and a gold star decorating their naked chests. About once an hour some of the waiters hoot loudly and race to the stage to do these little hoedowns that bring the crowd to their feet. The six guys on the stage, hands on hips and butts sticking out to audience, swirled their hips in dizzying circles. It was quite an attention getter. It certainly held my interest as they danced to a song I'd never heard — something about saving a horse by riding a cowboy.

The crowd went wild. Diners from the far end of the room, most with drinks in their hands, crowded closer to the stage. The waiters still working got mangled by drinkers cheering for the naked buttocks. It was like playing human-bumper cars when those little butts started twirling.

All the women cheered and clapped loudly. Beside them more than a few of their men viewed the dancers with longing and desire in their eyes, making the floor and the stage equally diverting.

When the entertainment ended and the crowd cleared out, I fought my way toward the Ladies. As I got to the end of the bar a voice called out, "Hey, Sherri."

I turned to see the guy calling my name. Built like a six foot five-inch tall fireplug, he was got up like a freak show. His graying beard was divided into sections and tied in bundles with elastics, the first elastic up tight against his jaw line and the second brightly colored band in the middle with a third at the ends, making thick packets of whiskers that fanned out from his jaw like a shield. His hair was pulled back from his face and tied in a long ponytail which was also bundled down its length with elastics in blue and green and red. Big gold loops adorned both ears. Wearing a Hawaiian aloha shirt, covered with yellow hibiscus on a black background, he looked like he'd dressed for the wrong party or had forgotten the theme. But you didn't hire a guy like Dix for his looks. It was all about muscle with him.

"Dixon Selby." I gave him a big smile. "Haven't changed your evil ways I see, still hanging out behind a bar."

Dix returned the smile, but then he always smiled like he'd just heard the best joke in the world. "And you, Sherri, still as beautiful as I remember and still enjoying the action."

"Every chance I get."

He picked at his Hawaiian shirt, pulling it away from his chest and shaking it to fan air over his body. "What brings you to Key West?"

"Lexi, and a little holiday. We went to high school together. Marley and I have been promising to come down for ages. We finally made it."

"Not going to work while you're here?"

"Not staying that long, only a few days."

Dix threw a towel over his shoulder, and leaned on the bar with both hands, his sausage-like fingers splayed. "Maybe we could have lunch or a drink or something."

The, "*or something,*" was what worried me. Dix was a predator. We had tended bar together at the Sunset five years back. The thing about being behind the bar with Dix was that he had the nasty habit of brushing up against you, as if the tight space had suddenly grown even more crowded and he couldn't avoid touching you. There was never enough abuse that you wouldn't feel like a fool complaining, but sufficient to make me want to take a bar knife to him. "Won't be time, but thanks anyway." Being up close to Dix was something I didn't care to repeat. I waved a hand and headed for to the Ladies.

"Hey, don't go." Dix was no longer smiling. He looked around to see if anyone was paying attention and then motioned me back toward him.

I went reluctantly.

He leaned toward me and whispered, "Don't tell." He leaned closer. His breath smelled of onions. I pushed back from the bar as he said, "I like Key West. No need for anyone to know about that other business."

The business he was talking about was being arrested for selling Florida snow. Somehow Dix had weaseled out of the cocaine bust and disappeared from Jacaranda without ever spending time as a guest of the state. My guess was he'd turned over someone more important so he could slide. He gave a languid shrug of his shoulder. "You know how it is. It was just so easy." He gave me one of his charming smiles. "I gave in to temptation."

I'd been doing my own share of giving into temptation. Lately all my nights had turned into sunrises, most served with tequila. My behavior had Marley barking at me like a chained dog at midnight, but I didn't like Dix and wasn't going to pass up an opportunity to slam him. "Life is full of temptations. Give in to enough of them and they become nothing but opportunities."

He straightened. A muscle in his jaw twitched. "If you tell Lexi, I'll be out."

It was true. Lexi would go ballistic. Crazy she may be but she was dead honest and expected everyone else to be the same.

That's when I saw the funny side of his situation. Dix liked sex the way other men like to breathe. "Working a gay bar has to be some kind of punishment for a straight guy like you."

His shoulders relaxed and his lips slithered into a sly grin. "I get my share." This was the real Dix, a piranha in trousers, always taking advantage and pushing the limits. "Thank God for tourists, right?"

"Whatever you say, Dix."

"Hey, did you and Clay ever get together?"

I thought I kept my face blank but he must have seen something because he frowned and asked, "Did I say something wrong?"

"Naw." I waved a hand and headed on to the next slice of insanity.

Chapter 3

Down the hall, I discovered another neat feature of the Rawhide Saloon. The toilets catered to all tastes, *Cowgirls*, *Cowboys* and one door marked *Undecided*.

While I was considering if I was truly committed or still undecided, the door directly across the hall opened as a guy exited the *Cowboys*, giving me a peek at the forbidden interior. There wasn't much to see except for a man dressed in black shirt and shorts, with a big silver cross on his chest, handing an envelope to another guy and getting what looked like folded bills in return. The door swung shut. But it didn't close before the guy delivering the goodies looked directly at me. The look he gave me was enough to send me scurrying for the safety of the ladies' room.

An elegant place of refuge, the western theme had turned bordello in here. Some upscale places give patrons extras — like hand cream. The Rawhide offered a basket of free pastel-colored condoms. Lexi had always been public spirited.

I worked my way back along the bar, watching the pours and trying to see anyone doing the dirty. There was nothing strange until I came to a beautiful woman pretending to be a hooker while turning down a date. "I'm meeting someone," she told the disappointed john. She didn't even try to hook up later. And then the strangest thing of all happened. After she got rid of the guy she bought herself a drink. She was the first working girl I'd ever seen who bought her own booze.

I slid onto the stool next to her, deciding I might just as well try and earn the drinks Lexi had been buying me. I leaned in close to her and said, "Hi." She gave me a slight smile but went back to studying the mirror behind the bar without answering. I asked, "How's crime?"

Her head jerked back so she could get a good look at me. Her nose curled as if I was emitting a foul smell. "Excuse me?" Some women have all the luck. While she looked to be in her early twenties from across the room, up close I was guessing she had another ten years on that.

"You heard me. Let's talk."

She swiveled her head to study the bottles reflected in the mirror — or maybe there was something else that needed watching. "I'm waiting for someone," she said.

I laughed. "Aren't we all? But we really need to talk. I'm Sherri."

She frowned, but replied, "Tanya." And then she smiled and started to snow me. I guess she thought it was better to talk to me while she kept watch in the mirror, than to keep brushing off guys who were looking for some action. She was blond and blue eyed and sweet, childlike almost, and trying hard to convince me how unworldly and innocent she was — a girl so dumb she'd take an IOU from a stranger with a bus ticket in his

19

hand. "I grew up on a farm in upper New York State," she told me.

I put my elbow on the bar and planted my chin on my hand. "No kidding. Did they grow corn there?"

"Yeah," as excited as a kid with a handful of her favorite candy, "How'd you know?"

"I'm a good guesser."

She pulled on the hem of her short leather skirt with both hands and wiggled on the stool in a failed attempt to pull it down. It did make for a good show. "Where'd you grow up?"

"Oh, I grew up on a farm in Florida."

She gave a little clap like we'd just found out we shared DNA or something. "What did your folks grow?"

"Cockroaches and mold."

Her forehead knitted into severe lines. Not so girlish anymore.

"Don't frown like that. You'll get wrinkles." I had one of those creepy feelings you get when someone is watching you. I looked down the bar and met Dix's glare. I told myself I was letting my imagination run away with me. Just another example of my paranoia. I turned away. "Does Lexi know who you are?"

Tanya's jaw hardened and the corn-fed mask slipped. "I think most people are better at minding their own business than you are."

"True, I've never been good at that, but if you're pretending to be a working girl there's a few things you should

20

know. You don't buy your own drinks and you don't turn down two dates in a row."

"Get lost."

"In a minute. Lexi has a little problem. One of her staff is skimming and I'd appreciate a heads up if you notice anything."

"Why do you think I'd be interested?"

"Crime is crime." Marley danced by with a guy dressed like a sailor. He may even have been one – if the Russian fleet was in. "Maybe you can kill two birds with one stone and catch a thief. That's what cops are supposed to do, aren't they?"

Her eyes darkened and the sweet little farm girl was replaced by a hard-jawed woman who looked like she'd like to hurt me bad. "Keep your wild ideas to yourself."

"Really, wild ideas? Dix, that weird bartender down at the end, isn't fooled any more than I am. So the person you're watching…" I shrugged. "You're not likely to fool him either. Perhaps we can help each other."

She slid off the stool and looked me directly in the eyes. "There's a bad storm coming. It might be a good idea for you to evacuate."

"No worries. We're only staying one more day. We'll be gone long before the storm hits."

"You may even want to go sooner. The emergency measures people are advising people to start packing." She proceeded to tell me how fast the storm was moving, what tack it was taking and where it was expected to hit.

I waved her words aside and returned to the only subject I was interested in. "Even if you're undercover, don't you have an obligation to help with other crimes?"

"Keep your drunken fantasies to yourself." She glared at me as she edged past me into the crowd, leaving her untouched glass of wine behind.

Never one to waste free booze, I picked it up and took it with me.

"Lexi, this is one heavenly place." The sweep of my hand may have been a little broader than I meant it to be. "Is everyone in here gay?"

She smiled and waved at an admirer. "I don't know. I haven't slept with everyone."

"Nice that you've learned restraint."

"Honey, I'm so restrained, I'm almost celibate."

"Now that I don't believe, but then no one here is what they seem." I looked around the room, taking in a hooker who wasn't and Dix the straight bartender in a crowd of guys who weren't. What other things going on weren't real? My glance shifted to the man I'd seen in the men's room. He was talking to a tired guy who looked like he drove truck, not the normal patron for the Rawhide. And he wasn't having any fun. It looked like it had been a long time since anything made him laugh. "Who's that?" I pointed at the guy dressed in black and wearing a giant silver cross.

"Father Pat, a good guy."

"Really?"

Something in my voice warned her. "What?" She turned to study him. "He was a priest. He was defrocked when he was caught on his knees praying to a different god, a much younger god."

"Hmm," I said and went back to watching Tanya the fake hooker snake her way through the bodies, taking the long road to nowhere, touching and smiling, always making contact but never hooking up. I pointed to Tanya. "Did you ever meet a working girl who wasn't working?"

Lexi grinned. "I saw you talking to Tanya. I didn't think your gate swung that way."

"Well, never say never, but it hasn't yet. Do you know her?"

"Yeah, a little. She isn't bright but she's a sweetie."

"The hooker with a heart." I clapped my hands with delight. "I knew she had to be out there somewhere. I swear, before I die, I'm going to see every stereotype going. And you might want to think twice about her mental capabilities. The best way in the world to put someone off guard is to play dumb and let their own sense of superiority snow them. I've done it a million times myself."

Lexi gave me a startled stare. "Oh, you mean that wasn't real?"

I shook my finger under her nose. "Dissing me is Marley's stick. Get your own."

"Hey, I just realized your initials, Sherri and Marley, stands for S and M." Her grin came and went in a heartbeat. "That's exactly what being around you two feels like right now. What in hell is going on with you two anyway?"

Maybe I wasn't the only one thinking this childhood friendship had come to the end of the road. "We're cool."

"Yeah?" Lexi said, "Well, please stay away from me when you're not."

I didn't want to discuss Marley. "I think Tanya..." That's as far as I got before she exploded. "Forget Tanya. Whatever is happening with her is none of your business. Just figure out who's stealing from the Rawhide."

"That's what I'm trying to do."

"Do you think you should be working the bar or something so you could see what's going on?"

Lexi was a genius when it came to marketing the Rawhide but totally naïve when it came to scammers. No grifter was going to do the business under the nose of the boss's friend. My plan was to convince the staff I was no one to worry about and I knew just the way to do it. Every bartender hates a sloppy drunk so that's who I'd be. Their disgust would work for me. One of them might even enjoy running a con right in front of me.

24

The trick would be to drink enough to convince them I was useless, but not enough to fall off my stilettos. Always a delicate balance.

I considered the line of tenders working the bar. Given his background, Dix was the most likely candidate for sticky fingers. I'd concentrate on him. He looked up. His menacing stare set off alarm bells. Something was going on with Dix. Perhaps his rage was because he thought I was filling Lexi in on his history. Whatever it was, he was not happy with me. More than that...but I couldn't put a name to the emotion.

Lexi snapped her fingers under my nose to bring my attention back to her. "If you've got any ideas, I'd love to hear them, Sherri."

"Give me a little time." I raised my empty glass. "And a little more to drink."

I leaned back as a waiter set down a platter of Hog Heaven ribs. I handed him my glass and burped louder than I intended. The story of that belch would reach the ears of every server in the room within minutes. They'd be feeling mighty superior after that, but what the hell, I was never going to see them again.

A vinegary aroma wafted up from the ribs and I breathed it in with delight. "There's enough here to feed a family of four."

"Excess, Baby, excess," Lexi said. "It's all about being over the top."

And looking around the room I saw it was true. It was all about excess. Everything was designed to excite the senses and take away any residue of caution, making you overspend and overindulge in all kinds of sins.

Marley arrived and I stood up so she could slide in to where her barely touched drink, with its melting ice, waited. "That's some kind of radar you have," I said. "You only show up when the food does."

Marley dropped a row of ribs onto a plate. She attacked the meat without even giving me the total of the drinks I'd consumed, but I knew she was counting. These days she was always counting. Marley pointed toward the dance floor with a rib and said, "Oh look Sherri, that lady is wearing your family motto."

I turned to look but the woman was already past. "What did it say?"

Licking her fingers, Marley said, "*Mess with me and you mess with the whole trailer park,* the Jenkins family slogan."

"Whoops, you owe me five bucks."

"What?" Marley protested. "I do not."

"You brought up that other world, reality, all the stuff." I stirred the air with my finger. "No reality for forty-eight hours… remember?"

"You mean you haven't even called the restaurant once? Isn't that why you snuck into the washroom straight off?" I didn't even attempt to deny it, but she hadn't been there so I wasn't paying. Marley added. "Can it survive without you?"

"Oops, another five bucks." I craned my neck, hoping to catch a glimpse of that shirt. "No reality, but I might need that tee."

"While we're at it, let's get one that says what Bernice always calls you, 'gutter trash and slut,'" Marley sniped. "That way you'll make lots of new friends."

"Friends of the best quality too. And they say it pays to advertise, but you owe me fifteen bucks now."

"What?"

"You brought up my darling mother-in-law... definitely too much reality, the trailer park and the Sunset. Anything else you'd like to say?" Fissures in our relationship had turned to cracks and then to deep crevasses that neither of us could cross. When we left Key West, we would likely be saying goodbye to more than Lexi.

Lexi wasn't interested in food or our squabble. She planted her elbows on the table and leaned towards me. "So, which waiter is screwing me?"

"It's more likely to be a bartender than someone on the wait staff. It's the guy in charge of the cash that's always the problem."

"See," Lexi said as though I'd actually told her something important. "You were always sharp on the uptake."

27

I laughed. "You obviously haven't been keeping up with my life."

Marley raised the rib like a baton, started to say something and then hesitated. Finally, she pointed her dinner at me and said, "That was very close."

Lexi's hand slammed onto the table. "Say, what's with you two?"

Marley and I grinned at each other, waiting for the other to speak. "You tell her," I said.

"No way, you do it."

I pursed my lips and shook my head. "I like drinking on your money."

Lexi slapped the table again, a sound loud enough to be overheard in the noise around us, another tidbit to be shared among the staff. The boss and her drunken friend were fighting. "Oh, for heaven's sake," Lexi said. "Are you two still at it? What kind of games are you playing now?" Lexi was really irritated, but Marley and I often have that effect on people. "Grow up?"

I smiled at her. "Now what fun would that be?" Marley ignored the whole discussion and went back to destroying the platter of ribs. "Marley and I are having a break from reality. Buy me another drink and I'll explain."

Marley said, "You better slow down or you'll never make it to closing time."

"Trust me. I've closed more bars than you've ever been in."

Marley laughed but there wasn't a lot of humor behind it. Oh yeah, our happy days were over.

Lexi frowned. "Be careful, Sherri. I left Adrian because of his drinking." Lexi's honesty wouldn't let the statement stand alone. "Well, that and the fact that he wouldn't leave his wife after two years of promises. He really loved me but he's a gynecologist and he thought coming out of the closet would hurt his practice."

The glass Marley was holding slammed onto the table. "Wait…" her finger waggled back and forth. "You… and he had a wife?"

"Yes, Marley," Lexi said. Her saccharine tone was lost on Marley. We watched Marley try and sort it out, her face showing her confusion. Marley's red curls were screwed up like a Brillo pad, and her freckled face was nearly free of makeup. She looked about sixteen. We were the same age, thirty-two, but I seemed to have aged two years for every one of hers. Now, when I looked in a mirror, I saw my mother's delicate features buried under bitter lines. Most of the time I've come to terms with no longer being the prom queen, but seeing Marley like this brought a flush of jealousy. I wanted to be as carefree and open as she was.

Marley screwed up her face in concentration. "You mean he's bi-sexual?"

"Yes, Marley." Lexi's eyes met mine. Her lips pursed, biting back the laughter. It was always amazing how much Marley didn't get, how innocent she truly was.

"It's like bifocals," I explained. "You can see double and have twice the fun."

"I just don't understand that." Marley took another rib from the plate. "Why get married if he was gay?" She started to take a bite and hesitated. She put down the rib, thinking it through. "Do you suppose his job did that to him? Maybe he was straight until he became a gynecologist."

Lexi spewed coffee all over the table.

"See why I love her?" I patted Marley on the head. "She is completely serious. My little dingbat."

"What?" Marley asked, her forehead wrinkled in confusion. "Did I say something funny?"

"Not you," I assured her.

Chapter 4

Before the ribs were finished, I looked up and saw Elvis striding toward us in all his glory. His white jumpsuit was studded with rhinestones and gold rivets. A white scarf flowed from around his neck. Nearing forty but hiding it well, his black hair was a shade Mother Nature had never designed. A handsome man, it would be hard to say no to him. Luckily, tonight I was in no mood for that word. Sure of himself, and reading pretty clearly my reaction, his dark eyes crinkled with humor. He grinned at me and drawled, "Hello, Darlin."

My insides melted. "Oh, you're good – very, very good."

Lexi said, "Hi, Jon," and tilted her cheek up to receive his kiss. They were the dream team in white, delivering memories of Marilyn and Elvis at the peak of their fame. I sighed, I'm sure I did, for all things lost and gone forever. While he leaned over and planted a peck on Lexi's upturned face, his eyes had already found Marley. She finished her conversation with a guy in the booth behind us and swung around. "Well, look who's back from the dead," she said. "And don't you look fine."

Elvis's eyes widened. He jerked upright. His mouth opened and closed. "Oh," was all he could manage. And then "I…." He swallowed and said, "You…"

Marley flung her arms wide. "Now that's what I'm talking about. That's how a man should react when he sees me, like he's just seen the one and only perfect woman, the woman of his dreams."

He grinned at Marley now. "You are the woman of my dreams."

"You mean nightmares, don't you?" I put in, not happy to be left out of the excitement. "Do you two know each other?"

"Nope," said Marley.

"Not yet," he said. "But we will."

I said, "Have you got a fever? Been feelin' dizzy long?"

"Shush yourself." Marley waved her hand, dismissing me. "For once in our lives a man is showing good sense and going for quality over quantity."

And he was going for her—staring at Marley like he'd found the Holy Grail. That charming smile flashed and he said, "Come dance with me." He reached out his hand and Marley took it. I slid out of the way as she rose gracefully to her feet to follow him onto the tiny dance floor. When they got there, Elvis took off his scarf and wrapped it around Marley, pulling her close to him while he murmured sweet words in her ear.

I leaned over to Lexi and asked, "What in hell just happened?"

"I think Elvis just met his Priscilla."

"Who is he?"

"Jon Kidd, an Elvis impersonator, he's working over at Rude George's doing four shows a day. Damn good, the best Elvis I've ever seen. We've been talking about booking him in here next season."

We watched and sighed, and maybe felt a twinge of jealousy, as Patsy Cline sang about pain and loss and Marley and Elvis danced, melting into one another, oblivious to the world around them. "You believe in love at first sight, Lexi?"

"Course, it's happened to me dozens of times."

"Yeah, that's what I think too."

They were making quite a show of it. A circle cleared around them. Marley was laughing up at him, enjoying the moment as she took the scarf from around her neck and held it out to her side like a matador enticing the bull. He circled around, answering her sexual baiting. And then he grabbed the scarf, and sweeping it around Marley, he pulled her to him.

"Did someone turn the temperature up in here or is it just me?" Lexi asked.

When the song ended, Marley and Elvis came back to the table. Marley leaned over with her hand out and said, "Hand me my purse. I'm going to Rude George's to watch Jon's show and a have a coffee afterwards."

"Oh, la la," Lexi trilled.

Marley laughed at her. "Not what you're thinking. Just a show and a drink. I'll be back before last call."

Chapter 5

While my commitment to sobriety was slipping away, Lexi grew more desperate as the night wore on. "Sherri, you have to help me."

"I can't see anything, Lex. I've been watching but it all looks good." I slid across the bench and started to stand.

Lexi grabbed my arm and held on like she expected me to run for the door. "If you can't find an answer, this time next week I'll be looking for a job."

"Easy does it, Lex." I pushed her hand away. "I may want to use that arm again." I rubbed my skin where her nails had bitten in. "You've got to take it easy on the workouts. You could hurt someone."

"I'll hurt you if you try walking out on me now." She had my arm again.

"Don't rush me." I peeled away her fingers. "You've had months to figure this out and you still haven't found an answer."

"I've wined and dined you, cajoled and petted you. Enough of the foreplay, let's get down to the real stuff. Who's screwing me?"

"Half of Key West would be my guess." I found my words outrageously funny but Lexi's face stayed fierce. I straightened. "Nice to see you haven't lost your sense of humor."

"Sherri." It was no longer Lex's sultry voice but the strident tones of a pissed off man. "There's something you aren't telling me. I know there is."

Had I let something slip about Dix? And why the hell wasn't I telling her about him? My intuition was telling me there was something going on with him, something bad. But it wasn't Dix I was concerned with, it was Lexi. She'd fire him and bring down a whole lot of trouble she didn't need. And she wouldn't be any closer to solving her problem if he wasn't the one doing the stealing. "I just need a little time," I assured her. "Don't worry."

"This isn't a game."

"I'll do better in the morning. Hard to concentrate this late at night."

"Stop trying to sidetrack me. You may convince other people that you're drunk, but your act doesn't fool me for a minute. You're as sober as I am."

It wasn't true. Somewhere along the line the act had turned into a certainty, but I wasn't going to share that with Lexi.

Lexi stared at the bar and her jaw hardened. "One of these bastards is costing me a lot of money." She stabbed the table with her forefinger. "What in hell is happening here? The paper keeps saying there's no crime in Key West."

"That's because it's all happening in the Rawhide."

"What do you mean?"

I wasn't ready to tell her about the priest selling drugs who was being watched by an undercover cop. And then there was Dix. Not for a minute did I believe that he'd been reformed. "The money lifting has to be something that doesn't take subtlety or finesse. Tell me about your accounting system."

She slid to the edge of the booth. "Come into the office and see for yourself."

Dix watched us go.

"Too bad your boss didn't spend as much on this system as he did on the décor. It's old style. You really need to update it."

"I know. This computer is almost as old as I admit to being. The owner was trying to save money and brought in one he had used somewhere else."

"Who has access to it?"

She looked startled for a minute. "Everyone."

"Well, that has to change. I've got a great system I'll sell to you cheap."

"Why would you do that?"

"I'm not going to need it."

"Why?" She watched me intently, waiting for the story.

I took a deep breath. "Big changes are coming. I've had an offer to buy the Sunset. I can't keep it going without Clay to help make the payments."

"So, that's why you're down in the dumps?"

"They're going to tear the Sunset down and put up thirty stories of concrete on the beach. That part of my life is ending, but it's still all I want."

Her face lit up. "Come to Key West, lots of bars here. And lots of work."

"Naw, I'm a Gulf kind of girl. Unlike most everyone else in the world, where I started is where I want to stay."

"That's just so boring!"

"Jacaranda is home and so is the Sunset."

"A bar isn't most people's idea of home. What's so great about it?"

I thought for a second. "I've watched the world revolve in the Sunset. From the latest movie to the town council's latest screw up, the big events and the small, all of them get discussed and judged. It's where my friends meet up, as much entertainment as it is my place of business. And…" I took a deep breath. "It's all I have left. I love the Sunset, love every rickety inch of it."

"Yeah, but how can a beat up old building, smelling of cigarette smoke and stale beer, wrap its arms around you and say, 'There, there, everything will be all right?'"

"It's a long time since a man wrapped his arms around me, despite what you may have heard from Marley."

"How long have you got to make up your mind?"

I sighed and headed for the door. "The offer is only good for three more weeks."

She jumped to her feet and threw her hands wide in a great exuberant gesture. "I know you're losing the Sunset, but a new life is just beginning. Start over, come to Key West."

"I don't want a change. I want my old life back."

She held the office door open for me. "That train has left the station, Hon. You need to move on. Life changes." She squeezed my hand. "It isn't the end of the world."

"No, but it's on the flight path."

Surprised by her laughter, I asked, "What?"

When she pulled herself together she said, "Marley says that sometimes you're not worth the trouble but you're always good for a laugh."

Chapter 6

I was only half pretending to be dead drunk when the ex-priest joined us.

I leaned an elbow on the table, prepared to begin an intelligent conversation, but somehow I slipped. Drinks were spilled. Father Pat, being a forgiving kind of guy, laughed and mopped up the dampness with sodden napkins that quickly became shreds. "I wouldn't want to have your head in the morning."

"Me neither," I replied. "Has anyone got anything for pain, OxyContin, Percocet, Vicodin?"

"Don't you love how Sherri is up on the latest medical news?" Lexi said. "The glamorous life of a bartender, socializing with hookers, drunks and druggies, she learns all kinds of interesting things."

"You know you're turning out to be a whole lot different from the fun-loving girl I remember." I waved my glass in her direction. "Shish is empty." Using two hands, I carefully set down the wine glass.

Lexi frowned. "You really gotta get a grip, girl."

"That's what I'm trying to do, get a drink and get hold of some pain killers." I turned back to Father Pat. "Florida is the land of pain killers."

Annoyance flicked across Father Pat's face, but when he spoke his voice was soft and gentle. "Why don't you just try something over the counter?"

I shook my head. Moving quickly was a bad idea. I grabbed hold of my head to keep from losing it. "Not as good, not as much fun. Don't you minister to any friendly doctors?"

A muscle jumped in the corner of his eye. "Nope. Don't know any doctors."

"Bummer. I like friendly doctors." I folded my arms on the table and laid my head down for a minute before jerking upright. "Wait, I got an idea. How about Holy water?"

"Sherri." My name exploded out of Lexi's mouth.

I grinned at Father Pat. "Will that work? Can you cure my hangover?"

He shook his head. "I doubt it. But a headache never killed anyone."

"That's the problem. I'll be praying for death a few hours from now but it won't come." I laid my head back down, but I watched him. "Still, you meet lots of druggies and people like that. If you meet anyone with the good stuff, remember me, will you?"

"I don't know anything about illegal drugs." He'd be a good guy to play poker with because every time he lied that muscle by his left eye twitched. You'd always know when he was bluffing. I should be starting a game. With him and the hooker, I could win a bundle.

40

A brilliant idea hit me. "Hey, if God made us, who made booze?"

Father Pat shook his head. "Looks like you'd know more about alcohol than anyone in the room. Why don't you tell me?"

"Yes, I've studied booze." I said. "Lovely stuff but I didn't make it."

"The other thing you aren't making is sense." Lexi was truly disgusted with my behavior.

Tanya danced by our table with a bald guy. She looked miserable. Undercover work didn't agree with her.

"You're supposed to lay them not sway them," I yelled at her. "Hey, everything I say tonight rhymes." This sounded like the funniest thing I'd ever heard and I shrieked with laughter, nearly sliding off the leather seat in hysteria.

Father Pat frowned and rose from the table. He nodded at Lexi and said, "Goodnight."

"Don't go. The night's still young." I reached out for his arm but he pulled it away. Oh, yes, I make friends wherever I go. And around us, people noticed the drunk, including two waiters. Oh, the stories they would tell.

Across the room, Dix watched. I said, "Did you ever wonder why bad things happen to nice people, Lexi?"

"Do tell."

"Because nobody picks on the meanest son-of-a-bitch in the room. They pick on the nicest. The lesson is, be the nastiest."

"What the hell are you talking about?"

41

"I have no idea."

It was nearly closing time. The bartenders were still working at a frantic pace. Everything still looked normal. I'd been watching these guys behind the bar all night and hadn't noticed one unusual thing. Most of all I watched Dix, sure that he was the one on the take. I would have bet my life that Dix would be running a game, but I couldn't see it. He had two blenders whirling while his right hand shook the martinis and his left hand set up the glasses. He didn't pay any special attention to anyone and didn't seem to have any interest in what was happening around him. He just methodically did his work. Had I made a mistake concentrating on him while someone else slipped by unnoticed? I was never going to figure out who was stealing if I didn't get closer. By now Dix had told the rest of the staff about me. Even believing I was drunk, they were going to be wary.

"Maybe you should work the bar tomorrow night, see if you can figure out anything that way," Lexi said.

"They'd just shut down until I was gone. No, we need to convince everyone that your drunken friend is no one to fear. I'm going to the bar. You follow me and we'll have a bit of a scene, tell me you aren't buying me any more drinks."

"Really? Do we have to?"

"Yup. No one's going to let me get anywhere near their light fingers if they think I'm going to run back to you with the news. Give me a minute and then come over."

42

Lexi waved away the bartender coming to take our drink order. "I'm listening. Explain."

"You and I are going to have a little disagreement and then I'm going to buy my own drink."

"Maybe the right person won't even see our little act."

"Trust me, the staff are all watching you like hawks. Everything about you and your friends interests them." I slid out of the booth and crossed the room using the backs of chairs to steady myself. It was a display that didn't go unnoticed. I was exactly the person every server hated, and with any luck I'd be the one nobody took seriously.

At the bar, the tenders were all busy. "Hey, Dix," I yelled, standing on the bottom rung of the bar stool and waving down the bar at him. It wasn't only Dix who paid attention to the drunk. "How does a girl get service around here?" It was humiliating, but effective. Every eye along the bar turned to me. Just to underline how obnoxious I was, I rapped on the counter. "Come on Dix, pick up the pace." People watched with disgust.

Dix was frowning as he came down the bar. "What's the problem, Sherri?"

Lexi wedged herself in beside me. "Don't you think it's time you called it a night?"

I waved her away. "No fun. Go away." I opened my arms wide to Dix. "Dix my favorite bartender." Suddenly the room spun and I slipped off the stool. Lexi grabbed me and stopped me from going down on my ass.

"What do you want, Sherri?" Dix asked when I was upright again.

"A little nightcap. Let's make it a double bourbon on the rocks."

"Make sure she pays for it," Lexi said, "because it isn't on my tab." She walked away. My fellow patrons weren't the only ones revolted by me.

"Screw her. Need a drink."

When Dix delivered my drink things suddenly looked different beneath the rearing stallion over the bar but I couldn't tell what had changed. I held my double carefully in front of me and stumbled off to find Lexi who was filling in for the hostess. "How many bartenders have you got working?" I asked, setting my drink on the shelf beneath the podium.

"Only three. I needed another tonight but no one was available. Two are driving over to the west coast ahead of the storm and Kevin is flying home for a holiday. He wasn't supposed to leave until Monday but decided to go early before the airport closes. Want to work the bar?"

"Not going to happen."

"Why not?"

"Because I'm going to make you a very happy woman. If you only have three bartenders working tonight, why am I counting four guys behind the bar?" I closed one eye and counted again. "Nope, not blind drunk — just drunk. There's still four."

It took Lexi a moment to see that there was an extra tender. "Oh, that's Skip, he's a waiter who used to be a bartender. He slips behind the counter when things get crazy."

"Well, isn't that nice." I laughed at the beauty of it. "The old kiss principle."

Lexi swung back to face me. "Kiss what?"

"KISS — Keep it simple, stupid. Skip is keeping it as simple as can be."

Lexi's face showed her confusion. "What? How?"

"Skip, even his name is nice and simple. Skippy." I made a grand gesture that nearly threw me on the floor. I'd misjudged. I was a little more inebriated than I'd meant to be.

Lexi pulled on my arm. "Straighten up and pay attention."

I stood straighter and held onto the podium so I didn't weave. "Why is he called Skip?"

"Short for Skipper, he lives on a boat. His real name is Paul Hyatt but everyone here seems to have a nickname."

"Nice. Jimmy used to live on a boat. But he's dead too. All the men in my life are dead."

Lexi gave an exaggerated sigh. "For God's sake, Sherri, let's not go there. Tell me what you figured out? Tell me about Skip!"

"He ish." My lips weren't co-operating. "Well sweet little Skip. The guy with the really cute…" I cupped hands and made circles.

Lexi slapped my hands. "Never mind his ass, tell me about Skip."

I concentrated on not slurring my words. "Sometimes when things get busy he slips behind the bar and starts mixing drinks."

"I just told you that." Lexi was about to burst. "He used to be a bartender but he'd rather be a server because he makes more money."

I nodded, my head going like a bobble head in a car window rather than something attached to my body. It wasn't the only thing out of control. I concentrated really really hard. "So, he mixes the drinks and he delivers them. He fills his own orders?"

"So?" She didn't wait for me to answer. "He isn't supposed to do that, I've talked to him about it, but it does help out at busy times."

"It helps little Skippity Do Dah most of all."

"What do you mean."

"Is a lot of your business cash?"

Lexi laughed. "Lots of people still don't want to be caught in a gay bar. They go to the ATM before they come in so they don't have the Rawhide showing up on their credit cards, on their expense account or even their own personal account. Nothing for the wife to be concerned about. They keep their tracks well covered."

"That's a bonus for Skip. You see, he doesn't put the order through the till until after he delivers the drinks. If they pay cash it goes into his chaps, if it's on credit card it goes through the register."

"Damn. I knew it had to be something like that."

"I've got a little idea how we can fix him."

Her hands curled into fists. "Me too, I'm going to break his neck."

"Settle down, Tiger. Gotta be able to prove it if you want to show the owner that you're innocent. You need this guy stitched up nice and tight."

I reached into my purse. Turning my back to the bar I defaced a dead president with my initials. "Call the cops and get a patrol car over here."

"What are you going to do?"

"Me? Why I'm going to go stick a needle in Skippy." I made a loud and embarrassing departure, leaving Lexi to deal with the scattered menus.

Chapter 7

At the bar, I waved Skipper over. "Lexi is being a piss-head." I held on tightly to the mahogany. "Lexi used to be more fun." It took two tries to get my ass onto the stool. "She's no fun anymore."

Skipper was model-thin and gorgeous, with olive skin as smooth and even as any teenage beauty. He smiled at my complaint but he wasn't going to get caught badmouthing his boss.

I tried to set down a nearly empty glass I'd picked up on my ragged path to the bar. It tipped over and spilled melting ice across the polished wood. I giggled. "I'm going to pay for this in the morning, but when has that ever stopped me from having a good time." He still smiled a tight little smile as he cleaned up my mess, but he didn't look impressed.

Lexi came up beside me. Planting an elbow on the bar, she stared at me. "Marley is right." She wasn't even trying to keep her voice down. "Your drinking is out of control."

"That's why people come to a bar, to drink."

"And you've done more than enough of that. You're drunk."

I stuck my forefinger in her face. "If I could stand, I'd walk out of here." That struck me as one of the funniest things I'd ever heard but I could see that Skipper wasn't smiling.

Nor was Lexi. She made a noise of disgust. "Well, it would be nice if you could get back to my apartment while you can still walk."

What a hilarious suggestion. "Too late." I shook my head. "And I'm having too much fun to leave."

Lexi turned to Skip. "If she wants another drink, she's paying for it." She left without waiting to see if I ordered one.

"She cut me off. Did she just cut me off?" I leaned forward so I could read the sheriff's star on his chest. "Did she just cut me off, Skip?"

"Seems like it." He wasn't even trying to hide his impatience. Talking was costing him money. "You want a drink or what?"

"Or what... what are you offering, Skippy?"

Skip grimaced. Annoyed and repulsed, he wanted to be away from the lush who was wasting his time. He nodded to the guy standing behind me and took his drink order, pulling two pints and taking the bill from the hand at my shoulder. He made change from the little leather apron slung low across his front. I watched very carefully as he tucked the bill away, but then I bet all the customers had their eyes fixed on that little leather shield. He started down the bar to fill another order.

"Hey Skippy," I called. He frowned, but came to stand in front of me. I waggled a finger back and forth and giggled. "No more free drinks for me, Skipporoni." I pulled out the twenty I had initialed, along with a crumpled tissue, and dropped them on the bar. I had a little trouble separating the two. "Bring me a Tequila Sunrise, an extra big one." And that struck me as funny as well.

When Skip set my drink and some change down in front of me, I swung around on the bar stool and lifted my glass to Lexi, standing at the entrance. Then I turned back to the counter and prepared to watch the action. I was curious to see just how badly Lexi would behave.

Lexi came back to where I sat and waved Skip over. Her voice was all barely contained fury when she said, "I need you in the office."

It didn't take a genius to see that she was infuriated. Panic swept his face. "Why?"

"I'll tell you there. It's too noisy here."

He came out from behind the bar, nervous and unsure, his eyes darting about trying to catch a hint of the trouble he knew was coming. I watched him closely, sure he might try to ditch the marked twenty, but then he didn't know it was marked, did he?

When he came out from behind the bar, Lexi took him by the elbow to keep him from bolting. I could see her long red nails dig into the flesh of his arm.

Skip winced. "Hey, you're hurting me." He tried to shake her off.

"That's nothing to what I'd like to do to you, you little shit." They marched for the office at double time.

I pushed my glass away and followed, but not as quickly or as steadily.

There was another person in the room when I slipped through the door. I nodded at him and he dipped his head in acknowledgment.

Lexi grabbed Skip's shoulders and spun him around to face her, saying, "You've been stealing from the Rawhide."

"You're hurting me."

Rather than let Skip go she shook him viciously. "You little piece of excrement, I've been taking grief for your crimes."

The uniformed cop stepped forward and removed Lexi's hands. "That's enough. I'll take over now." He held Lexi back and looked to me. "I'm Officer Panebianco. What do you know about this?"

I told him. When I was done, he said, "I'm going to search you, Mr. Hyatt. Do you have any weapons on you or anything that might harm me?"

Couldn't the cop see that Skip was nearly naked? Where was he going to hide a gun? My nasty mind was twirling with possibilities.

"Remove your apron, please," the officer said.

Tears welled up in Skip's eyes. "Please, Lexi, don't do this."

"You're just lucky the cop is here to protect you, Dickhead. If it was up to me you'd be on your way to hospital, not to jail."

Skip undid the leather apron. The cop turned it over to reveal the small pocket that had been added to the inside. My marked twenty was there. "Paul Hyatt, you are under arrest," Officer Panebianco said, and read Skip his rights.

Tears streamed down Skip's face. "I'm sorry, Lexi. I needed the money."

"Don't say anything," I warned Skip.

Lexi swung around to face me. "Whose side are you on?"

I raised my hands and backed away.

"Lexi, please, I'll pay back everything." Skip reached out to Lexi, pleading, "Don't let them take me to jail. Do you know what will happen to me there?"

"Begging doesn't mean squat to me. You almost got me fired. Did you care about that?"

The cop ignored the bickering but I was betting he had taken note of Skip's confession. When he started to cuff Skip, Lexi yelled, "Wait. He's not wearing that outfit to jail. I want it back. Make him take it off."

The cop glanced down at Skip's bare bottom. I swear, that big hunk in uniform looked terrified. "Does he have anything underneath?" he asked, stealing another quick peek at Skip's nether regions.

"No." Lexi folded her arms across her chest. "I want that uniform. Let him go into the staff room and get dressed."

The cop took off his cap and used his forearm to wipe his brow. "All right. I don't want his bare ass on the seat of my cruiser, but I'll wait outside the door while he gets something decent on."

Now that that was sorted, Lexi turned to me and threw her arms around me. She hugged me until I yelled for mercy. "I love you," she said and grabbed my face in both her hands and planted a kiss on my lips. "Love, love, love, you!"

I was pushing back from her but she held on tightly. "Lexi," I yelled. "You're hurting me."

"Sorry." She eased up but still didn't let me go. "You are a very clever bitch."

"Hey, I didn't go all the way through the eighth grade for nothing. But don't make too much of it."

"Why?"

"It's best not to have things to live up to because I'm much better at living things down."

"Still a clever bitch."

"It's just that I've seen every act at least twice. They can put a new twist in the tail but it's still the same old kink."

"You're clever and funny." She kissed me again. I saw the cop grinning at me.

Dix was waiting when I left the office. Maybe not waiting as much as trying to listen. There was a brief flash of…. what? Anger? Or was it fear?

"What's up?" he said. He crossed his arms and waited for me to answer.

I edged away from him. "Everything's good." He was looking for a fight and I wanted no part of it. "No problem," I said, trying to reassure him.

He nodded to the door. "I saw a cop go in there."

"Yeah, you did, but it's sorted."

He relaxed a little. "And Skip, what about him? What story is he telling?"

"He's under arrest."

"No shit!" He laughed out loud and his arms came uncurled. "You mean…" he laughed again and stroked his beard up where it joined his chin. Relief softened his face and he was the happy-go-lucky guy again.

"Why…" I started to ask what he thought was happening but stopped myself. I didn't want to know. In twenty-four hours, I'd be back to my own reality. No need to get involved in anyone else's. In the meantime, the night was young and I was going to have some fun.

I sat with my new best friends, a group of guys down from Michigan who were flying out in the morning and were in the mood to party.

One guy loved to dance. There's nothing as sweet as a man who likes to dance. We were two-stepping around the floor to some Texas music when I saw Father Pat talking to a tall thin man. The guy didn't belong in a tourist bar. He looked like he'd be more at home on a fishing boat pulling in nets. The leathery skin of his face was stretched tight, another man who hadn't smiled in a long time. I watched over my partner's shoulder as the man got up and walked away with an uneven gait that favored his right side. He left the saloon without ever buying a drink or glancing at the bare backsides. His only interest had been in finding the good father. Tanya followed the tired man out the door. I was sure she was outside flashing her badge at him and turning him into a witness, bringing more pain into his life.

Lexi had to get control of this. Just like keeping rats and cockroaches out of your building, in our business you need to be vigilant about people. The last thing you want is a drug dealer setting up shop in your bar. It brings in the wrong crowd and chases out the ones you do want.

But I'd had enough of other people's problems.

Dancing: that's pretty much all I remember from the remainder of the night. Oh, that and getting up on stage to perform with the lovelies in the chorus line but hey, who can resist dancing when Shania is singing, *"I feel like a woman."*

I didn't notice that Marley hadn't returned. Didn't know she hadn't made it back for last call.

Chapter 8

Friday, 72 hours before Alma hits

The next morning, I didn't feel like a woman — I felt like a bag of shit. I laid there on the couch and contemplated death, sure that it was better than being conscious. The rooster that woke me crowed again. It's an unpleasant sound to hear when your head is throbbing and your stomach is doing backflips, but in Key West it's a sound you need to get used to because the town is full of feral chickens. In the old days, cock fighting was a big form of entertainment. When it was banned the owners of the fighting stock opened their cages and chased the birds out into the gardens and pathways of the town. With no predators, they thrived and multiplied in the jungles of live oak, palms and giant ferns. Now their descendants roam all over Key West. Why hadn't someone put them on a grill like my Daddy did with the feral pigs back in Jacaranda?

The rooster crowed again. If I had my way that bastard would be dead before he could ever wake another person. Then again, my stomach would have given me the wakeup call if he hadn't. The smell of coffee made it worse. I groaned and fought down bile as I kicked off the covers.

I got cautiously to my feet, praying I wouldn't embarrass myself before I made it to the bathroom.

"Well, look who's still alive." Lexi's voice drilled a track of pain through my skull. "Didn't die of alcohol poisoning, then?"

I slowed my dash for the bathroom and risked turning my head to where she sat at the small metal bistro table by the front window. I tried to smile and show I was doing fine – no harm done. It probably looked like the grimace on a death's head. I waved a hand and stumbled to the bathroom to hug the toilet and pray for death.

Lexi threw the door open. "Kneeling before a higher power is a step on the road to enlightenment."

"Piss off."

She handed me a damp facecloth. "How about some bacon and eggs? A bloody Mary? Eggs Benedict?"

I tossed my answer into the bowl. She shut the door.

My head was throbbing and my legs were like rubber, but I'm no quitter. I joined her in the living room. Lexi looked up from the newspaper she was studying and said, "Marley and I are going to hit every sale in town this afternoon." The gorgeous woman in white from the night before was gone. Dressed in grey sweats, with no makeup and her hair pulled back in a ponytail, my friend Mason peeked out from his hiding place. "Want to come with us?" she asked.

"While I'm trembling with anticipation at the thought, I think I'll pass." My sandpaper throat put gravel in my voice.

The humor left her face. "Are you all right, Sherri?"

"Doing great." I sat down at the table. "I think I managed to convince all your employees that your friend is no one to worry about."

"All of Key West, I'd say. You'll go down in the history of outrageous and that's saying something in this town."

I felt myself wince but I wasn't crumbling before her disgust. "Anything worth doing is worth overdoing."

"Well, I really appreciate your going over the top, or in this case, over the bottom, on my behalf, but I'm starting to think Marley is right, your drinking is out of control. She wants to do an intervention."

"So she told me on the way down. Who in their right mind picks Key West to talk about sobriety?" I brushed my hair back from my face. "Marley doesn't get that fear and loss can't be packed away like out of season clothes. She just thinks I can wake up one morning and decide to move on."

"Maybe you should get some help," Lexi said gently.

I've heard that enough times to make it old news. "What finally happened with you and Adrian?"

The change in topic didn't fool her but she went along with it. "It didn't end well, but then none of my romances ever do." She rose and ambled into the kitchen area and poured more coffee. "His wife behaved very badly when I broke the news of our affair to her."

"Ouch. How bad was it?"

"Attention getting."

"Why is it," I asked, "that all our relationships start with kisses and flowers and end with tear gas and a swat team?"

"Because we're special." She studied my face. "You aren't going to hoop again, are you?"

I pushed myself upright, paused to see how that would go, and then wobbled carefully to the couch. "I need to catch up on my rest." My hip sank into the crack between the two cushions that felt like they were stuffed with stones. I pulled the sheet over my head to block out the cruel light. The front window was open slightly. The blind covering it went tap, tap in the breeze — like a woodpecker drumming on my head. My stomach rolled.

I kicked the sheet onto the floor and rolled off the couch and stood up. The room became a tilt-a-whirl.

Lexi said, "Becoming an alcoholic is easy when you're a bartender."

"Don't worry. I'm not a drunk. Although I may have flirted with it this last bit."

"Flirted?" Her voice rose to the register that only dogs can hear. The sound pierced my brain, drilled right through to the frontal cortex and set my grey matter screaming for pain killers. "Last night you didn't just flirt with it: you got engaged, put on the ring and set the wedding date."

"I'm astounded by your generosity in sharing your opinions." I carefully made my way to the bathroom. "Now is there anything more you would like to say before I go kill myself?"

In the bathroom, I scarfed a handful of pain killers and waited to see if they were going to stay down. Back on the couch, sheet over my head, I was still debating if my stomach had stopped cycling through the reject setting when Lexi said softly, "Are you sleeping?"

I growled, "No, I'm painting the ceiling." These days the words that flew out of my mouth were often more bitter and harsh than I meant them to be. Kindness seemed to have died in my soul. I didn't blame friends for giving up on me. Hell, I'd ditch myself if I had a choice.

I heard a door shut. I slept.

Chapter 9

The apartment was quiet when I awoke a couple of hours later. I figured Marley and Lexi had gone shopping. I was glad to find myself alone in that little upstairs apartment. The coffee in the carafe was as thick and black as tar so I poured a large glass of water and took it down to the veranda.

I stepped outside into a damp wall of heat. I stood there for a moment, trying to decide if I'd retreat to the almost air-conditioned house.

While the rest of Florida is all about sunshine, in Key West it's all about finding shade. Plantings on top of plantings filter out the hot sun and make the overgrown front yards into jungles of live oaks and palms, hidden and romantic. Bromeliads, in bright colors, decorate the trees. Color is everywhere, on the houses and the plantings. Flowers and greenery spill onto the sidewalk and huge bougainvillea climb up buildings and over trees, covering everything in orange and red and fuchsia. The houses themselves are mostly Victorian gingerbreads painted in pastels and look more like delicate Victorian wedding cakes than wood and mortar. Too little land on the island means these houses are built on top of one another with tiny front yards, often behind white picket fences. In Old Town, some houses are so close to the sidewalk that it seems you can reach over the pickets and shake hands with the homeowner, sitting in a rocking chair on his porch, without even needing to open the gate and walk up the old zigzag brick path.

This white gingerbread lady with a silver tin roof, where Lexi rented the top floor, was the exception to most of the homes with their small front yards. This one was set back twenty feet from the street. Lush palmetto sheltered at the base of a massive oak tree. A giant stag horn fern, about four feet across, hung from the lowest limb of the oak. Orchids, blooming in every color, also hung in baskets from the limbs of the oak. A deep veranda ran across the front of the house, private and quiet. It was the perfect place to hang out and recuperate from my excesses.

I sunk into a deeply cushioned chair, upholstered in a yellow trellis material. More white orchids bloomed in big terra cotta pots on every flat surface on the veranda. It was a special place to spend a lot of time. I watched as a marmalade cat slipped under the front gate and into the garden. It stalked through the giant ferns, freezing in watching mode every few seconds. Along with chickens, Key West has an abundance of feral cats. Some people say they come from Papa Hemingway's pets, at least the cats with six toes.

The screen door behind me crashed open and a woman shot out. She picked up a basket of stones and started hurling them at the fleeing cat. "Run, you damn thing," she yelled after it as it bolted under the gate. She saw me sitting in the deep shade of her porch. "Oh," she said, setting the basket down. She

62

frowned. "You must think I'm awful but I can't abide them digging in my gardens and doing their business." She smoothed her hands along her ragged shorts. "You never get rid of the smell."

I climbed to my feet the way Marley's mamma had taught me. "Yes, ma'am, I can see how that would upset you. You have a beautiful garden." I held out my hand. "I'm Sherri Travis, I'm a friend of Lexi's."

She stepped forward and firmly shook my hand. "Petra Bishop." Bare-footed and above seventy years of age, she was a walking cadaver. The bones in her face jutted out under her skin, her nose a sharp arrow. With her baggy paint-stained shorts, she wore a washed-out lime green t-shirt. Bright red reading glasses were perched on her head, her hair pulled back in a long grey braid. She lowered herself into a white wicker rocker and said, "Those damn cats. I love my garden but it's not a spot for children, large men, or cats. They just break things and stink up the place."

Hard not to laugh.

The rocker was going at a furious pace. "I guess I shock you. Some people get nicer with age, but not me." Her hair and her skin had been brutalized by too much sun, but in her faded blue eyes a light still shone. She wasn't dead yet. I was betting she hadn't even contemplated that situation. "Never going to be one of those sweet old ladies you see in ads." More furious rocking. "I love my plot of earth more than I do people."

"It looks like a botanical garden."

"I've tried to put in a little of everything, but there isn't much room." She pointed to a huge shrub, twenty feet high with leathery green leaves, growing at the corner of the veranda. "At night in the summer, when that frangipani is blooming, it's like heaven out here." The chair creaked with every pass, a strangely comforting sound. "In Hawaii those pink and yellow flowers are used to make leis."

"Your orchid tree is about the biggest I've seen." The forty-foot tall tree blossoming in the side yard was covered in giant purple flowers that were shaped like butterflies. "It's about the only tree I can actually identify. My grandma had one in her yard."

We sat in companionable silence until her frank eyes met mine. "Lexi told me about you, about your loss."

A nod was all the acknowledgement I gave this statement. "Your house must be one of the original Key West Houses."

She smiled and nodded as if we'd reached some sort of agreement. "My grandfather was a wrecker. Do you know what they were?"

"Yes, ma'am. These treacherous waters and the Florida reef took hundreds of ships, broke them up. The wreckers were ship owners who would race out there and get the trade goods off the boats before they sank."

"You're putting it kindly." Her face softened with her smile. "Some say that a few, like my great grandfather, lured the ships onto the rocks and scuttled them so they could steal their cargo." She shrugged. "Maybe it was the strong currents that drove the ships onto the reefs or maybe it was something else. I don't know, but the men in my family were salvaging ships up to 1910 when the courts put them out of business. Stripping floundering or sunken boats still happens, only now it's called marine salvage."

I laughed. "I guess that's what my dad's doing right now. He's out in the Gulf of Mexico looking for a Confederate ship that supposedly sank with a load of gold onboard. He's spent his life hunting for it. Personally, I think it's a myth."

"Well, we all need a dream, something to keep us going. I guess this garden and house are mine."

I rubbed at the dull ache in my left temple. "Are you worried about the storm coming?"

She snorted. "My great grandfather, Nathaniel Bishop, had this house built about 1870. These old houses of Key West were built by ship's carpenters, which is probably why they've lasted so long. They were constructed to withstand the worst that nature can deliver. They're all permeated with salt, preserved and polished by it, just the same as us Conchs. This house has been battered by a hundred tropical storms. If the winds don't go over a hundred miles an hour, she'll do fine. I'm staying put. I'm not leaving my house to the looters. But the tourists will leave. Other fools will rush down here to see the big wind."

"Won't the police keep the storm chasers out?"

"They try. Tomorrow the police will have a blockade up on Highway One, stopping people from coming down. But the storm chasers always find a way. You can't stop stupid. We'll have flooding. They won't like that. Won't like it when it's ninety degrees and the electricity is out and mold starts to grow everywhere and they can't get off the island. Unfortunately, the storm is going to coincide with high tide. They're expecting a coastal surge of eleven feet, enough to wash those fools wanting to get up close and personal with Alma all the way to Africa." She smiled with satisfaction. Her grim little beam said they'd only be getting what they deserved. "Can't see why they enjoy someone else's troubles."

"Well, Marley and I are leaving real early tomorrow. The worst winds won't hit until well after that." I drew in a deep breath of silken air. The light is different in Key West, not like anywhere else I've ever been, brighter and clearer. "Hard to believe there is any threat today, isn't it?"

"Today is a peach. It won't be long before the wind picks up and then we'll have rain but I'd trade the tourists for the wreckers and storms any day."

I laughed. "You sound like my dad. He's always grumbling how tourists are ruining Florida and lamenting how much better things were before he was shipped to Vietnam."

She turned from studying the orchid tree to face me. "Your dad and I have lots in common. I was a nurse in 'Nam."

"That must have been pretty horrible."

She snorted. "Only if you don't like being sent into a war zone unarmed."

"Did you stay that way?"

A wry grin pulled at her thin lips. "What do you think?"

A gecko darted half way down the post holding up the roof, saw us and stopped, head up and considering the situation. We watched his red throat throb. Nearby someone was smoking a joint. The pungent odor smelled like home.

I wanted to stay right there on that veranda for a very long time.

Chapter 10

Lexi came in and said a brief hello as she passed us. I took my time following her upstairs to apologize.

Lexi was at the table madly writing. She ignored me. The smell of fresh coffee wafted through the room. I filled a mug, keeping my back to Lexi so I could hide my trembling hands.

I took my coffee over to the table and watched Lexi, who was all glammed up in skinny jeans, form-fitting top, and impeccable makeup. I probably looked like I'd just survived a train wreck. I sipped my coffee while I waited for her to acknowledge my presence.

Finally, she lifted her eyes from the papers spread out in front of her. "Are you feeling better?"

"Sure." But I didn't want to talk about me. "Is Dixon Selby down here in Key West fishing for square grouper?"

"What's square grouper?" Lexi asked.

"Bales of weed."

I had her attention. "Why are you asking me that, Sherri?"

"He had a reputation for selling blow in Jacaranda. Not likely he's given up his sideline. And square grouper used to be the fisherman's best friend in Key West."

"Shit." Lexi's frown deepened. "But there are no drugs coming into Key West anymore. The papers say that all the time. It all goes right to Miami."

I shrugged. "I might be wrong but I thought drugs might be what brought him here."

"One more reason it's good to have someone like you around." She rose gracefully from the table and went to the sink, running hot water over her mug to rinse it. She turned off the tap and put the coffee mug in the rack to drain. She swabbed off the counter vigorously and ran the dishcloth over the taps.

"Say it or you'll burst," I told her.

She wrung the dishcloth until the spots screamed. "What makes you think I've got something to say?"

"If you were a book you'd be a grade school primer... real easy to read."

She smiled. "I'd rather be something racy." She tossed the cloth into the draining rack. "I do have something on my mind." She took a deep breath before she continued. "You know everything there is to know about running a bar. You see things I don't, understand things I miss." She dried her hands over and over on a tea towel while staring me down. At last she said, "There's this pub on Duval Street called the Running Dog. It's packed to the sidewalk every night. The Running Dog is for sale. I've been thinking about it all day. I can't afford it on my own but together you and I could do it. Things are ending for you at the Sunset and it's time you tried something new." She stared

69

intently at me and asked, "Do you want to buy the Running Dog with me?"

"Whew." I slumped back on the chair, letting go of the tension that the thought of another lecture had delivered. "That's a surprise."

She rushed to the table, planted both hands on it, and leaned over me. "You already said you can't afford to keep the Sunset without Clay and you've got an offer on it. I can't afford to buy this on my own. Together we could clean up."

"It might be true," I said, cautiously. "It depends on what they want for it."

She pushed the papers she'd been working on toward me. "It's all here." She jabbed her forefinger on the numbers she'd worked up. "I tried to tell you about it this morning, wanted you to go with me to see it, but you were busy painting the ceiling."

"Sorry."

She brushed aside my feeble attempt at an apology and said, "I can raise my half."

I drew the papers toward me and looked at the numbers and then I gave a whistle. With the sale of the Sunset I could raise my share. Even better than that, there'd be no more mortgage and no more worries. A life line, that's what was on the table. What was holding me back? "Just let me look at the numbers and think it over."

Her face dipped into despair.

"I'm not saying no; I'm just saying I have to think about it. There's absolutely no one else I'd ever consider doing this with." *Except Clay,* that rotten little voice in my head added. Loss surprised me at the strangest times. I ducked my head so Lexi couldn't see.

Lexi wasn't fooled. "I know life has kicked you around." Her voice was gentle. "This is a chance to start over, a new life."

I nodded. "A new life would be nice. Lately, mine hasn't been worth living and if it doesn't pick up soon I'm not sure I can hang in for retirement."

She jerked upright. "Sherri, you aren't talking about..." Bouncing on her toes with shock, she couldn't even say the words.

"Naw." Easy enough to say. "I'm fine." I couldn't tell her about my dance on the edge of crazy, about doing the shimmy with panic and fear, barely making it through the long nights. Self-medicating with alcohol was the least of my problems. Most nights I didn't make it out of the bar, sleeping in the office and going to the gym in the morning for a shower. I only went to the place I'd shared with Clay to pick up clean clothes. But there was no need to tell anyone about that.

"Key West is a good place to live, welcoming and safe." She gripped the edge of the table in her eagerness to convince me. "Despite Skipper, there is very little crime here."

"Speaking of which, you realize of course that Tanya, everyone's favorite hooker, is an undercover cop."

71

"What?"

"Didn't you figure that out?"

She shook her head.

"She's new to town, right?"

"Yeah. She's only been here a few weeks."

"There you go. New cops always get put on undercover as soon as they arrive."

"How do you know?"

"Long story."

She pushed her fingers into her temples as if she could help her brain take it in. "First I have a waiter cheating me, and a bartender who may or may not be a drug dealer, and a hooker who is an undercover cop? Anything else?"

"Father Pat is dealing drugs."

"How do you know this stuff?"

"Experience – a lifetime of it." It was true. I grew up in the roughest, nastiest trailer park you can imagine. Sure, there were some nice people there, but most often they were the victims of the drunks, sociopaths and criminals who controlled the Shoreline and committed crimes against the other residents. Fights, and violence of all sorts, were daily events.

A policeman I know once told me that he was a human garbage man. He picked up human garbage so nice people didn't have to see it. Being raised in a trailer park on the edge of a swamp, I saw lots of human rubbish. It made it easy to identify it when it showed up elsewhere.

How many kids from that collection of broken down trailers ended up in jail or dead of an overdose? Most. I got lucky. On the first day of grade school Marley and I decided to be best friends and over time I became the sister she never had and she was the sister I didn't know. Her family gave me an iron-clad example of a normal family and a home where there was no screaming, no plates being thrown and no threat of violence. Her mother and father treated me like their own child, taking me in on weekends and holidays when my own mother was working. Only trouble was, their life was as boring as piss, but at least I knew that drunken brawls, child neglect and gunfire weren't how the average person lived.

The Shoreline taught me something invaluable. It educated me in paying attention. Sometimes I overreact to situations, screaming, "Back off," without waiting to see if it is needed. Growing up, Marley's mother, a mother to me as well, was always telling me to be nice, but I knew, deep in my soul, being nice marks you as prey and no place on earth is so safe you can let your guard down.

Lexi seemed to read my silence. "Maybe Key West would be too quiet for you."

"Oh, no. I want a quiet life."

She leaned back and laughed as if I'd just told her the best joke in the world. "Who are you kidding? You get off on trouble. Always have, always will. Like women are attracted to the wrong kind of guys, you get hot for trouble. When others run away from it, you hustle forward to embrace the beast."

"Bullshit!"

Lexi shrugged. "Whatever. Think about moving down here, that's all I ask." Lexi patted my hand. "Tonight, as a thank you for exposing Skip, I'm taking you to the Running Dog for a drink. And then, I'm taking you to Newtown for a giant steak."

"Great," I said. "I haven't eaten all day. I need a little meat."

Lexi said, "Don't we all, honey, don't we all."

"Where's Marley?" I looked around as if I could have missed her in the tiny apartment. "Is she getting ready?"

Lexi gathered up the papers from the table. "Marley didn't come home last night."

Saying the sun had died would make as much sense. "What the hell are you talking about?"

"Just what I said." She looked over her shoulder at me, surprise at my reaction showing on her face. "She isn't here."

Chapter 11

The crowded little second bedroom belonged to Lexi's roommate who had gone north to visit family. With every inch of wall space covered with male pinups, and rank with the smell of cheap scent and hairspray, it was oppressive. The only window, tiny and looking out onto the side wall of the house next door, was covered in lace curtains with more pictures pinned to them. Yesterday I'd had a look at them, pictures of attractive men in various stages of undress. Now I saw all this again, but what I didn't see was Marley.

Baffled, I looked around the room, sure that somehow I'd missed her, but there was no purse, no shoes kicked off at the door, nothing to say that she'd come back to the apartment.

I swung around in a circle. "She isn't here!"

"I told you, she didn't come home last night."

The dependable center of the universe, that Baptist-Dudley-Do-Right who never wavered, had failed. My joy at Marley's fall from the goodness pedestal faded as quickly as it came. The sun didn't fail to rise, and there was no way anyone veered this far from their center — especially not Marley. A new and nasty thought formed in my head and in my heart. "Something's happened to her." I can't say why I was so sure, but I was. "It must have."

Lexi gave a dismissive shrug. "So, she stayed over at Jon's." Her smile was one of affectionate confusion. "I don't understand. Why are you making such a big deal of it?"

"You think it's normal for Marley to sleep with a guy on a first date? You think it's usual for her not to come home? You and I'd do that, but not Marley."

"Honey, we all do it."

"Not Marley. Our Onward-Christian-Soldier girl has never pulled out her roots. She has rules for how long she has to know a guy before she goes to bed with him and I can tell you it's a lot longer than a couple of hours. She has to know both his mamma and grandma by their first names."

"Ah, but this is Elvis." Lex grinned and did a head jerk towards the living room. "Check your cell."

Hope went off like fireworks and I sprang for my phone. "Come on, come on," I yelled as I waited for it to get up to speed. There was no message from Marley. I hit her number. The call went to voice mail. I flopped down on the couch.

Lexi came to join me. "Marley is a big girl. So what if she spent the night with Jon. Why has that got you bent out of shape?"

"You don't understand. She's all about doing the right thing and she always knows what it is. And Marley would never not call. She checks in until you go mad. She should be here. Back by last call, that's what she said."

"She'll be all right."

"No, she won't." Why I was absolutely sure of this statement? "You and I are survivors, but Marley is an innocent. And she believes the best of everyone, believes everything she hears. Even a commercial convinces her. Do you have a number for Jon?"

"No."

"Why the hell not?"

Lexi gave a startled lurch. "It's not like he's a friend, just a guy passing through, a guy I was thinking of hiring. I have his bio and his agent's number at the Rawhide."

My panic wasn't doing any good. I fought to speak in a calm, sensible voice. "Can you call someone? Maybe he's at work, call Rude George's."

"Not open yet."

The smell of coffee permeating the small living area made everything seem so normal, but the world had been upended. I lowered my head onto my hands and thought hard. There had to be a logical explanation that I hadn't thought of, but none came to me. Nothing. I lifted my head and watched dust motes dancing in the sunlight streaming in through the window and tried to find an answer. Panic grew. "We need to talk to Jon. Can you find him?"

Lexi picked her phone up from the charger on the window sill. "Someone will know where he is, hard to hide in Key West." I jumped to my feet wanting to do something, anything. Trouble was I couldn't think of one possibility so I paced. Lexi only made three calls before she got Jon's number. She punched it in. It took some time for him to answer. I listened to her end of the conversation and knew Marley wasn't there.

Living through hell begins with an uneasy feeling, a question that can't be answered, and then it gnaws away at your core until the truth slowly eats into your being. Still you don't accept it. You squirm around and try to find some other certainty. I'd been down this road before. I knew what was to come and was starting to pant with anxiety. I took long slow breaths and fought for control.

Lexi was frowning when she hit the End key. "He says they went for a coffee and dessert after the show and then they picked up a pedicab outside the restaurant. Marley dropped him at Rude George's for the last show and kept the cab to come back to the Rawhide. They're supposed to be having a drink before you leave tonight."

"He said we're leaving tonight?"

"That's what he said."

"We're leaving tomorrow morning."

"I can only repeat what he said. He hasn't seen her since she dropped him off before his last show."

"So, from about ten last night until this morning she's been gone, not at the Rawhide or Rude George's, just gone?"

"It would seem so, but the whole island is only four miles long and two miles wide. She couldn't get lost."

"So, where is she?"

"There must be a simple answer."

"And what's this simple answer?"

Chapter 12

Something was wrong, very wrong. I grabbed my purse off the scarred end table. "I'm going to the police."

"Wait." Lexi held up her palms to stop me. "Call them. It will save time." Lexi handed me her phone and went to get the small directory from the top of the fridge. "Here's the non-emergency number." With her finger on the page, she read it off as I dialed.

The cops didn't want to know. Seems they have rules about when they start looking for people. "She's an adult, she's entitled to her privacy," the officer told me. "Until your friend has been gone for seventy-two hours, we won't take a missing person report." The voice on the phone was calm and reassuring, his tone saying, "there, there, dear." I couldn't make him understand that Marley would never leave willingly without telling us. It was inconceivable. "Your friend will come home on her own. They always do."

I wanted to curse and heap abuse on him. Instead I took a deep breath and said, "You don't understand. She doesn't know anyone here."

He wasn't impressed by that argument either. "Let me tell you a little story so you will understand how things happen. There was this guy whose family called us and reported him missing. They were all upset, claimed he would never do anything like this. Well..." He gave a wheezing little laugh. "Seems he went to a party on a yacht, had too much to drink and fell asleep somewhere inconspicuous. The yacht left Key West with him on board. It was about twelve hours later when he woke up and realized what had happened. He tried to talk them into turning around without any luck. I think he finally ended up in Boston. His poor family was going crazy." I tried to interrupt but he wasn't finished with his good news. "Miss, you gotta realize that every day in the U.S. there are as many as one hundred thousand people reported missing. Most of them come back on their own."

"She told someone that we're leaving Key West today. She's in a hurry to leave. I think she wants to get out well ahead of the storm."

"Well, there's your answer, and it's a good idea. Alma is getting stronger and moving faster with each passing hour and we are directly in her path. No one will be allowed down the Keys after today and the cruise lines are already rerouting their ships."

"So, don't you think this would be an unusual time for her to go walkabout?"

"It's our experience that people do unusual things when they're on holiday. They show up a few days later all contrite and embarrassed, but none the worse for wear. Perhaps she's already left Key West, by plane or boat, hitched a ride ahead of the storm."

"Leaving her car and clothes behind?"

"She'll call you soon and tell you all about it."

I said, "Perhaps you should check that, airplanes and such."

"If we checked up on everyone who someone thinks is missing, we wouldn't have time for anything else. If your friend is still gone tomorrow, come and see us."

"Tomorrow? She could be dead by then." I wished I hadn't said that out loud. This evil thought was followed by another. Maybe she was already dead.

"Try the hospitals," he said. "And call us in the morning."

"Hospital…yes." He had already hung up.

It didn't matter. I had a fleeting sense of relief, maybe Marley had had an accident. Crazy to think that her lying unconscious in a hospital could be a good thing.

Lexi was already looking up the number for the hospital. "Here it is." I punched in the numbers as she read them out. No one named Marley Hemming was a patient there, nor was there anyone of that name waiting in emergency. No unidentified persons were in the hospital, in fact most of the patients had been evacuated ahead of the storm. Only a skeleton staff remained. Could Marley somehow have got caught up with the evacuees?

"We need help," I told Lexi as I dug out my cell. I didn't want to make this call but it was all I could think to do. I turned my back to Lexi and listened to the ring tone. It went to Styles's voice mail. "Hi, it's me…Sherri." As if he wouldn't recognize my voice. I took a deep breath and told him what the problem was. "Can you just call the cops here and see if you can get them moving a little faster? I…" No use saying anymore. "Thanks." Before I even hung up, I realized a hard truth. There was no one going to help me find Marley, not Styles and not the Key West police.

"So, is that the cop that Marley told me about, the guy she saw you giving mouth to mouth before Clay died?"

"Trust Marley not to leave out any of the good bits."

"So, what happened?"

What had happened? I still hadn't made sense of it. "It was late at night after my dad's birthday party. I went into the kitchen to make the coffee and Detective Styles followed me with a stack of dirty plates." I dropped my phone into my purse. "Strange, that's how I always think of him." I ran my fingers through my hair, gathering it together and pulling it into a pony tail. Before I could pick up the hair tie from the table, memories stilled my hands. "We have a tangled past and that night in the kitchen, with Ella Fitzgerald singing *Summertime*, when he took me in his arms and we slow danced it was like it had always been destined to happen. He kissed me." It was more than just a kiss. I'd clung to him like he was my life raft. "It was a perfect moment … until Marley pushed open the swinging door. Our passion would probably have lasted no longer than a manicure. We…well, no use talking about that. Marley got upset, made too

83

much of it, thought it meant that I was cheating on Clay and was about to have an affair with a married man. She won't let it go."

"So, there's nothing between you and this Styles?"

"Nothing."

"But Marley thinks you're having an affair and it was going on before Clay died?"

"There was never anything between Styles and me." Not quite true. Sometimes the heart knows things it never tells, believes in dreams that will never be, and desires possibilities long dead. Sometimes, we just want more than one thing, desire something we can never have, hold gold and reach for brass. I could never explain that to Marley who always saw life in simplistic terms. My only defense had been that life was confusing. "Well, not mine," she'd replied. She'd never made a fool of herself over a man, never lost control. That's why her being missing didn't make sense.

I wrapped a tie around my hair. "I'm going to Jon's place. Where does he live?"

"No idea."

"Call him back."

She tried but Jon wasn't answering.

I grabbed my purse off the chair where I'd dropped it. "We have to find him."

Lexi nodded. "I'll make some calls."

"In the meantime, I'll check downstairs." A desperate idea gave me momentary hope. "I've got the key to the front door. She couldn't get in and maybe she didn't want to wake us. She's probably sleeping in her car." It suddenly seemed so obvious.

Lexi shattered my joy. "But it doesn't explain where she's been this morning and why she didn't meet us at the Rawhide and why she hasn't called. Doesn't explain why she's still sleeping at this hour of the day."

"Maybe she woke up and decided to go for a walk or get something to eat."

"Lame," Lexi said.

Chapter 13

Logic didn't defeat me. I ran down the stairs. There was no one on the porch. Marley's Neon was parked on the street where we left it. I hurried out to check on it. No Marley and nothing in the Neon that hadn't been there when we locked it up the night before. As far as I could tell it hadn't been moved.

I went back to the veranda and walked around to the side entrance. I hesitated before I knocked on the lime green door.

When it opened, I said, "I'm sorry to bother you, Ms. Bishop."

"Petra." She opened the door wider and moved aside. "Come in."

I stepped into a kitchen from a museum. Everything, from the floor to the ceiling, was made of dark wood. The cupboards all had brass latches that belonged on a ship. The only relief from the dark wood was a pine table that had two matching chairs with lime green gingham cushions. Sheltered from the sun by trees, the air was much cooler in her kitchen than it was upstairs where the window air conditioner was working its heart out.

I searched for Marley in the shadows of the room that smelled of lemon polish. "Have you seen my friend Marley?"

"No." There was an unspoken question in her voice. She cocked her head to the side, waiting.

"It's just…" I was suddenly embarrassed to admit to this grey-haired woman that Marley hadn't come home, sure that Petra Bishop would be making all kinds of moral judgments. She looked like one of my old aunties, who were eager to be scandalized and sure I was capable of it. But this was no time for false niceties, no time to pretend what wasn't true. "She went out on a date last night and didn't return."

Her body jerked straighter. "That doesn't sound good." She pulled a chair out from the table and pointed at the one in front of me. "Sit." When I did, she planted her forearms on the table and said, "Tell me everything."

I explained the situation. She thought about it for a minute and then she started asking all the right questions. "This isn't normal behavior for her?"

"Never."

"Does she know anyone else in Key West besides you and Lexi?"

"No." But my brain was saying that wasn't quite true. "She might know Dix. Yes, she knows Dix, but he's scum."

"Could she have accidently met up with this guy and spent the night with him?"

"No way. She wouldn't go near him. Never." The idea was ridiculous. But then so was the idea she had disappeared.

"Still." She lifted her shoulders and let them fall without saying anymore.

I nodded in agreement. "I'll check with him."

"Could she have met someone else she knew and gone somewhere with them?"

"Possible, but why wouldn't she bring them to the Rawhide or at least call to say she wasn't coming?"

"I have no idea."

And that was the problem, neither did I.

"Does your friend do drugs?"

"Never! Not even pot. Being drug free is like a religion with her."

"Alcohol?"

"Very little."

"Meaning she isn't passed out somewhere?"

I shook my head. "Did you hear anything last night, hear her come in?"

"No, I only heard you." Her lips twitched in a faint smile. "Quite a singing voice you've got there."

"Yes, I make up in volume for what I lack in talent. Sorry."

She waved my apology away. "I like to hear young people enjoying themselves."

Young! When had I last felt young? I picked at my thumb nail and tried to think what else I could do. Petra rose from the table and went to the window over the sink. She pulled aside the curtain. "Storm's coming."

I didn't want to think how that would hamper Marley's return. "It's a perfect day out there."

88

"I know. It looks even better than yesterday, doesn't it? The weather before a storm is always deceiving, tricks people into staying when they should be running. But the barometer is falling and there are swells over ten feet out there. The wind is right behind those waves, maybe thirty-six hours left but not much more." She let the curtain fall and turned back to face me.

"A real dumb time to do a disappearing act," I said.

"She wouldn't have run from the storm?"

"Leaving her clothes and car behind?"

"And you're sure she doesn't know anyone here?"

"As I said, only Dix, but she wouldn't waste five seconds on him."

"Still, it's somewhere to start."

Upstairs, Lexi was still on the phone trying to track down where Jon lived. It took twenty more minutes to come up with an answer. Lexi finally hung up the phone and said, "He's renting a house over by the cemetery."

"Let's go." I was already on my way to the door.

"Give me a minute." She went to her bedroom. The door was slightly ajar.

I called out. "Petra says we should check out Dix because he's the only other person Marley knows on the island."

"He was on the bar all night. It was busy and I sure as hell would have known if he'd ducked out for even a minute." She came out of the bedroom with a giant shiny black purse over her shoulder and pulling on a faded red baseball cap, a thing I would have sworn she would never own.

"Let's swing by Dix's place and see what he has to say."

"I don't know where he lives, but I have his number." Lexi pulled her pony tail through the back of the cap. She took her phone out of her bag, scrolled through her contact list, and then handed me the phone. Dix answered as I was stepping out onto the veranda.

When I told him why I was calling he said, "I never saw her after she did that dance with Elvis. Don't try and get me tangled up in this shit." Dix was always over-confident, sure of his own superiority. That's not what I was hearing from him now. Now he sounded worried, frightened even. "I don't want anything to do with whatever you've got yourselves into. Don't go bringing any of this down on me."

"Look, I'm only calling because you know her, so if you see her, call me. Or Lexi. You have her number."

"I won't see her."

"I know you'll want to help us find her."

"I can't help you. Goodbye."

I stared at the phone in surprise at his reaction. What had I expected? Concern certainly and an offer to help, but there was neither of those. Something was going on with Dix, but did it have anything to do with Marley? More likely it was his fear of coming to the notice of the police. I'd made the mistake of focusing on him and nearly missing what was happening with
90

Skip. Now I had to be sure not to overlook Dix because I was certain Elvis was responsible. What if...

"Sherri." Lexi brought me back to the present. "What did he say?"

"Says he never saw her again after she left with Elvis."

"Did Marley know Jon before last night?"

"If she did, why wouldn't she say she knew him?"

"Maybe this is all a joke. You two haven't been getting on so well lately. Maybe she..." A shrug was all she had left.

"Wants to teach me a lesson? She disappears like this so I'll.... what?" I walked away.

"Wait. I have to tell you something."

I knew from her voice I wasn't going to like it. I turned to face her, my gut tightening with apprehension.

"Jon knew about Marley."

"What do you mean? What did he know?"

"He saw her picture. He came into the Rawhide last week to talk about playing here in the fall. I showed him that picture of you and Marley on my phone, the selfie you took in the bar last week. He seemed real excited by that picture, said that one of you looked just like someone he knew. I told him your names but he said he didn't know either of you." Something in my face must have told her what I was feeling because she raised her hands to me and said, "You can't blame me for this. I didn't do anything wrong. I was just so pleased that you all were coming." She lowered her hands. "I've got a real bad feeling 'bout him."

I didn't tell her that she wasn't the only one.

Chapter 14

Lexi's pink scooter was a bit of a revelation. I would have expected a fire-red sports car. With the big shopping bag purse on her lap, she sat with her back straight, hands on the handlebars, like some crazy ad for scooter life, and drove with great concentration like someone's granny. Her caution amazed me. Hadn't her whole life been one big risk? And yet her driving was the complete opposite. Maybe her life wasn't about throwing caution to the wind and going to extremes so much as it was about doing the only thing possible for her. Strange, while I never needed to take risks, I always pushed things to the limit. And Lexi, whose whole life was all a risk, was basically careful and sensible.

Four blocks from Lexi's apartment, on the opposite side of the street, I saw Tanya open a gate and start up a brick path to the side entrance of a house. I had a good look at the house and memorized the number so I could find it again.

We coasted sedately past the house on Wrecker's Lane where Jon was staying. It was a narrow street in between Passover Lane and William Street, but there was nowhere to park even a scooter. We had to go two blocks down and walk back to Jon's place. Like all the others on this short street, the pink stucco house had been built in the fifties. Sadly neglected, plants grew out of the eaves along the edge of a roof that needed replacing. The concrete block underneath the stucco was showing through the thinning finish. Low and long, with deep overhanging eaves and jalousie windows to let in the air and filter the light, it had glass block panels on either side of the front door.

A black SUV was parked in the weedy driveway. Heat radiated off the side of the vehicle as I cupped my hands around my eyes and tried to see in through the tinted windows. I couldn't see much, but there seemed to be nothing that might be Marley's and nothing that could be Marley herself, no huge bundle that could have a body inside. *Why are you bent on thinking the worst?*

Lexi tugged on my shirt. I followed her to the front door. Fall leaves and a dead gecko had drifted into a pile at the edge of a brick planter. The front door, made of cheap plywood, was delaminating in long strips, exposing raw wood beneath the faded turquoise paint.

It took Jon a few minutes to answer my pounding and even then he opened the door just wide enough to see who it was. He frowned and closed the door a little more, bracing it with his shoulder. "I told Lexi everything I know about your friend."

He was dismissing Marley's disappearance and our fears as if he'd played no part in it. Right there and then my temper started getting the better of me. "Let us in," I said, pushing on the door. "It's us or the cops."

His jaw tightened. "There's nothing more I could tell them. I'm sorry she's missing but I have no idea where she is."

"Open the door." I pushed harder.

He kept his shoulder against the door but stepped back a few inches, not trying to keep us out but not inviting us in either. "I don't know where she is. How many times do I have to say it?" In the daylight, the roots of his black hair were auburn, nearly red. Dressed in cargo shorts and a pink golf shirt, he no longer looked like Elvis but more like the guy next door who mowed his lawn every Saturday morning before taking his kid to his little league game.

"Let us in," Lexi said from behind me. "Just to talk." She put her hand on the door just above mine. "Please, Jon." Emotions flashed across his face. He wanted to keep us out, but he also wanted to placate us. "Please," Lexi said again.

His body slumped in resignation. He stepped back. I pushed past him into a bright lemon yellow living room, a room someone had decorated when the house was built and then forgot about. It was the kind of retro room Marley would go mad for, but it wasn't the decor I was interested in. "Where's Marley?" My eyes searched for any sign that she had been there – a glass with her lipstick on it, a crumpled napkin, some small possession, anything. There was nothing, and the mid-century modern furniture didn't allow for hiding places. I could see under and around the sparse furniture. "Marley," I yelled. If she was there I wanted her to know that I would find her. Or maybe I was just yelling out of fear and frustration. "Marley!"

Lexi made soothing talk, trying to cajole Jon into helping us. "Sherri's really worried. She thinks something might have happened to Marley."

"That's awful, but I have no idea what it could be." His voice was full of concern. He glanced from Lexi to me. "Maybe she had an accident on the way back to the Rawhide. Did you try the hospital?"

I went through a little arch in the wall to a small dining room that opened into a kitchen where dirty dishes covered the counter and filled the sink. There was no sign that Marley had ever been in this room either and there was no place to hide an adult.

"Hey, what do you think you're doing?" Jon said. He followed me into the kitchen and jerked me around to face him. "You can't do this, can't just burst in here and go anywhere you like." A red flush crept up his face. "Listen to me. I don't know where Marley is. We had a coffee and she left. That's all I know."

He tried to push me back to the living room. A deep pit of anger that I'd been tamping down for months exploded in me. I banged my weight into him, knocking him backwards. He hit the counter and a surprised look flashed across his face. The tiny voice of reason that sometimes still hung out in my head told me I was being irrational. I didn't care. I was no longer concerned with embarrassment or hurting someone else. Those were emotions for people who had never known desperation and loss, people who didn't know that there was only one fleeting second when disaster could be averted. "If only"…those were words I never wanted to use again. Back through the living room, I rushed down the hall, heading for the bedrooms.

Jon followed. "Who do you think you are?" he roared, coming up close to me. I could smell the funk of sweat and coffee on him. "What have you done to her?" I yelled in reply.

Lexi tried to separate us. "Wait, wait," she said, stretching out her arms and using her size to push us apart. With her back to Jon, blocking him, she held her palms up to me. "Wait a minute, Sherri."

"You wait. I'm going to find Marley."

"This isn't helping." But Lexi was wrong there. It was helping me. I needed something physical to do and, more importantly, I needed someone to blame. "Let's just talk like reasonable adults." She turned to face Jon. "We aren't accusing you of anything, Jon." She had him trapped up against the wall with her body, her hands on either side of his head. It was strangely intimate and unless he really wanted to get nasty he wasn't going anywhere.

She started going over things with Jon, almost serenely, still looking for a logical explanation. As she asked sensible questions, I opened the door of the first bedroom. It had two single beds, covered in tropical bedspreads, with a solitary night table between them – but no Marley.

Jon yelled, "Hey, stop that."

This room was too tidy to be used and there were no human odors. It smelled flat and dead, not the way a room smells when people spend time there. On the other hand, the window on the far wall was open about three inches. Maybe that's why it didn't smell like anything. The open window held my attention. Why would the window be open if the air conditioning was on? Silly question but my brain was in overdrive. I was running out of time. Jon and Lexi were pushing and shoving at each other, working their way down the hall toward me. The closet was empty except for a couple of plastic bins. The only thing to see under the beds was dust and an old shoe that had been there for a very long time.

Next was the bathroom, pink tiles and a pink tub that was rusting around the edges. Hair and face products littered the counter and back of the toilet. There was no shower so there was no curtain to hide behind and there was no sign of Marley.

Down the hall I opened the last door and stared at the chaos of the room. The smell of unwashed sheets and dirty laundry was overpowering. Unlike the rest of the house, this room was cool. There was an old-fashioned air conditioner in the lower half of the window. The rest of the opening was blocked by plywood. An empty suitcase was open on the bed and clothes covered every surface. The white jumpsuit hung from the track above the open sliding door of the closet.

There was a loud thump that sounded like a body hitting drywall. "Shit," I heard Lexi say. I lunged for the bedcovers spilling onto the floor, intending to lift them and have a look under the bed, but Jon caught me from behind. With an arm around my waist and his other hand buried in my hair, he pulled me back toward the door. His unshaven cheek scraped mine and he hissed in my ear, "You're not going in there." I yelled for Marley while I fought, fingers raking his face, my arms and legs flailing. His spit splattered my face. "Get out of my house." He threw me into the hall.

"Why? What don't you want me to see?" The one clear impression I had of the room was the open case on the floor and the pile of clothes on the bed. He was leaving.

Chapter 15

Lexi was there again, separating us and holding me in place.

Jon danced with anger, shaking a fist at me. Blood trickled from his nose where my head hit him. "I don't have to prove anything. I didn't do anything." He wiped away the blood with the back of his hand. "If Marley is really missing, I'm sorry. But I hardly know her, only met her a few hours ago, why would I have anything to do with her disappearance?"

"What do you mean, really missing?" I asked.

"I can see how she might want to get away from a crazy person like you."

We stared each other down. He was nearly as irrational as I was. He flapped his hand at me. "Get her out of here."

Lexi said, "We've done enough here." It wasn't true. It was not nearly enough. She grasped me by both shoulders. She was bigger and stronger than me, and she could take me easily. "He's going to call the cops if we don't get out of here."

"That's fine with me." I wasn't worried about being arrested and charged with disturbing the peace. I was past caring about future problems. I just wanted to know that Marley wasn't in that house, that I wasn't walking out and leaving her behind. I put my palms up, trying to soothe Lexi and to sound reasonable. "Why won't he let us see in there? There must be something he's hiding."

"Sherri, he doesn't have to let us see in his bedroom."

I started calling, "Marley, Marley," over and over at the top of my lungs, wanting her to know that we were there, that we'd find her and we weren't giving up.

"Oh, for god's sake, get her out of here before I have her arrested for assault as well as trespassing."

Lexi's right arm went across my shoulders, holding me tightly to her. "You can't do Marley any good if you're in jail." She led me into the living room and said, "Look, we're just concerned, Jon. Just tell us about last night, tell us when you last saw Marley." She held me tightly to her and waited.

"Okay," he said, nodding his head as he straightened his clothes and smoothed back his disheveled hair. "Okay," he said again. "I would have told you straight off if you'd asked. We went to the Il Paradiso for coffee." Now that his hair was smooth, one palm brushed against the other as if he was dusting off any misunderstanding. "You can ask there." The tone of his voice was sure and confident. "Wait," he said, raising a finger. "I have proof." He went to the coffee table and picked up his wallet. "I charged it, coffee and dessert." He sorted through the billfold. "Here." He held out the receipt and I took it. "Look." He jabbed a finger at the strip of paper and said, "See? We were there. The waiter will tell you." He smiled. "A tall redhead as beautiful as Marley is unlikely to be missed."

The date and time were on the bill. "So, you were there," I said. "Then what?"

101

"We grabbed a pedicab and went to the club. I had to do the midnight show. She dropped me off and took the cab back to the Rawhide for last call. Just like she said she would." It came out easily, as if there was nothing in the world for him to hide.

"Why her?" This was something I'd asked myself on the way over, why he had chosen Marley — not that she wasn't lovely to look at, far from it, but his reaction had been something else, something over the top. Was there was some set of specifications she met, some need in his mind that she filled? Some perverted sexual thing was all I could come up with. *Don't go there*, I told myself and tried to wipe that thought from my imagination. "Why did you take her? Was it because she looked like someone you knew?"

"That's crazy talk."

"You told Lexi she looked like someone you knew."

"Not really, not when I saw her."

"Then why? She isn't rich, so it's not a kidnapping for ransom. White slavery? Did someone, somewhere, order a redhead?"

His face flushed crimson and his eyes bulged. "Listen, you crazy bitch..." He snatched the receipt out of my hand. "Don't go talking that trash to me." His fingers fumbled, trying to stuff the paper back into his wallet. "Get the hell out of my place."

"Sorry, Jon, sorry," Lexi said, pulling me away from him. "Just tell us the rest."

"There isn't anything more to tell." He walked away, slapping his wallet against the palm of his left hand, trying to get control of himself before turning back to face us. "That's the last time I saw her. She dropped me off and I went to work." He tucked the wallet away and looked me directly in the eye. "You can check. I stayed there until closing time. Lots of people saw me."

"Why are you packing a bag?"

His eyes shifted. A small tell of discomfort. Tiny, barely imperceptible, but it was there. "My gig is up next weekend. The tour boats aren't stopping because of Alma, so no tourists." He blinked, and then he seemed to regain his confidence. "Everything is closing. I'm getting out ahead of the storm... going to do some shows up in Orlando." He relaxed, shoulders coming down and his weight shifting to the right side. He was in his comfort zone with his story. I didn't want that. I wanted him mad and out of control so he would slip up.

"Who's going with you?"

"No one. Just me."

There was only one place he got freaky. "So why did you pick on Marley?"

Fury jerked him back into a fighting stance. "Get out."

"I told the police about you. They'll be coming. You won't be able to hide. You can't get away with this, Jon. And if you escape from them, I'll find you."

"You crazy bitch, you can't threaten me..." Jon pulled his cell phone out of his pocket and waved it at us. "Get out or I'll call the cops and tell them there's a crazy woman in my house."

"Fine," I said. "And when they get here they can search your house for Marley."

"I have no idea where she is. I never saw her after I went to work."

Strangely enough I finally believed him, which meant Marley had been missing longer than I thought. "What did you do before going to the restaurant?" It was a crazy question and I had no idea why I asked it except that he'd kept emphasizing he hadn't seen Marley after the pedicab. Maybe something happened earlier which didn't really make sense if he was seen with her in the restaurant.

"I'm done talking to you."

Lexi pulled me to the door. "Sorry, Jon," she said, and shoved me out through the door she held open.

With the slam of the door I realized there was one question I'd forgotten to ask.

Chapter 16

The sun radiated down on us. A flock of green parrots flew into the live oak across the lane – just another perfect day in Paradise. I sat down on a brown patch of grass that had been peed on by a hundred dogs. "We should have stayed. Let him call the cops. Every second takes Marley further and further away from ever returning. We need to get back in there."

"Why are you so sure Jon is behind this?"

"He was the last person to see her."

"Was he? What if she left him just as he said? What if someone else kidnapped her?"

Lexi had a point. But I wasn't done with Jon yet. "Call the police. They need to search that house."

"You know the police don't consider her missing. They are not going to search anyone's house." She tugged on my arm to get me on my feet. "He's watching us from the window. Let's go." She pulled me down the sidewalk. "Jon may not be involved. And the more time you waste on the wrong person, the less chance you have of helping Marley."

I stood still. "It's just too bizarre to believe that he came into the Rawhide, saw Marley and reacted like that, and then someone else took her."

"Maybe it wasn't like that."

"Then what was it?"

Lexi grimaced and turned her back to me.

I put my hand on her shoulder. "What?"

"I can barely think it, let alone say it."

"What?"

"What if she was knocked down by a car, a hit and run, and no one's…"

It was not what I expected. "Jesus, Lexi…" But was that any worse than what I was thinking? The truth we both had accepted was that something bad had happened to Marley.

Tears moistened her cheeks. "Let's just go," she said and started walking away from me.

"Not until I see what's out back." I'd been so focused on Jon and what was inside his place I'd only just thought about the exterior of the house. I headed in the opposite direction from the scooter. "Along the rear of the houses is a narrow lane. I noticed it when we went around the block looking for a parking space. I bet we can see the back of the house from there. Let's check it out."

She sighed. "Okay. Let's go have a look out back and then we are getting out of here."

We went to the end of the block and around the corner to the alley with Lexi trailing well behind me. Short, with only a dozen houses backing onto it, the alley was from an era long before municipal planning. The narrow walkway was now being used for garbage cans and junk that didn't make it to the dump.

"Maybe it's private property," Lexi said, looking back over her shoulder for someone official to chase us away. Ahead of us two brown chickens scratched at the crushed oyster shells that made the path.

Lexi stepped delicately through the discards, dog shit and the odd used condom, saying, "How can people let things go like this? It's disgusting. This is what comes from homeowners who live somewhere else and buy properties just to rent out."

I shut out her rant and tried to figure out which one was the back of Jon's house. I stopped at the fourth house. In the filtered light of the overgrown backyard it was hard to know if I had identified Jon's house or not. While the front of it was pink, this side was a faded yellow.

"This is it."

"Are you sure?"

"It's the fourth house."

"But it's not pink."

"They didn't bother to paint the back of the place." It looked abandoned and unloved, the yard strewn with rubbish. "This is the one. See that open window? That's the second bedroom, the window was open when I looked in there. I bet I could get into the house that way."

Lexi yanked me around to face her. "What are you talking about?"

"I didn't really check out every room. What if she was locked in a closet or under a bed?"

"You can't be locked under a bed.'

"Wouldn't you think there would be a utility shed?"

"Why?" Lexi answered. "No one ever cut the lawn here."

A man and a dog came down the alley. He nodded and started to pass but then stopped and had a good look at us, memorizing our faces for when he called the police after the break-in.

"Watch it," I said, pointing to his dog. "He's into something nasty there."

He jerked the poor little dachshund off his feet. "Leave it, leave it," he said, yanking the leash again for good measure.

"Let's get the hell out of here before he calls the cops," Lexi whispered, starting to follow the man and his dog.

"Wait, let's see where this goes." I started down the lane hoping to find a second way out, but now I saw the reason for the funny narrow track. It dead ended in front of a tiny little cottage, painted in a bright turquoise with purple trim and shutters. It was surrounded by a high chain link fence. The gate was padlocked. No way out except the way we came in. If anything went wrong I was trapped. But what could go wrong?

"Watch the front, Lexi, and let me know if Jon leaves."

"You aren't going in there, are you?"

"Naw."

"Liar." But she didn't argue, just waggled her butt around to the front of the house.

A mocking bird sang from the thicket of green. It was hard not to think of the heat and how uncomfortable I was. I shook out my tee, trying to get a little breeze. From the front of the house came the sound of a car door slamming. Was Jon leaving?

He had an afternoon performance but if he was taking Marley somewhere off island, it was unlikely he'd hang around because of a show. Maybe I shouldn't wait to go in the house. I checked up and down the alley, making sure I was alone. Jon could be gone by dark, and with him, Marley — *if Marley is still alive*. I forced that postscript out of my head. I would go around and see if Jon had left. If he had, I'd go in now and see if Marley was there. If not, I'd come back after dark. I tried to memorize the yard so I could get around it if I had to wait until dark. There were no motion detector lights but nobody cared about robbers in this back yard. There would be a full moon tonight. The radio had made a big deal of Alma arriving at a full moon and high tide.

The window was too high for me to get in without help. I examined the yard for something to stand on. There was a glass table, overflowing with empty beer cans, sitting up close to the house. They'd make a terrible racket if I hit them or tried to move the table. Beside the table an old wrought iron chair leaned at an odd angle. If it would hold my weight without collapsing, the chair was my best chance. But would it give me enough height to get through the window?

109

"Sherri." Lexi stood at the mouth of the lane frantically waving me toward her. When I had nearly reached her, she speed-walked away. I ran down the rest of the alley. I caught up with her half a block away and joined her in what was for me extreme exercise.

"What's wrong?" I asked, huffing along beside her.

"Jon saw me. Then he pulled out his phone and started to punch in numbers. I think he's calling the cops." She kept on walking while she talked. No trouble breathing there.

I said, "Calling the cops is a good idea."

"Oh, yeah? If they arrest us, we can't help Marley. Let's go around the block to the scooter."

Lexi was taking a bigger detour than necessary but I didn't complain, although by the time we got to Passover Lane I was begging for mercy. Lexi didn't slow down until we were on Margaret Street at the entrance to a cemetery. A sign said the huge gates were locked every night at seven. Bent over at the waist, hands on my knees, trying to breathe, I managed to ask, "Why do you lock the dead in at night?" Sweat dripped.

Lexi, checking behind us for cop cars, didn't even look at the iron fence with its forest of concrete blocks and granite spires. "A Key West tourist attraction, there's a hundred thousand people buried in here and we only have 30,000 living residents in all Key West. They've got us outnumbered." She looked back over her shoulder in the other direction, expecting to see a police car.

110

I stepped into the gap between the open gates. Some of the concrete boxes were only a foot above the grass while others were shoulder height or even higher. "But why put them in concrete apartment buildings?"

"In 1846 a hurricane washed away the old graveyard. Apparently, there were bodies all over the place so they reburied them here, but this time above ground —nineteen acres of dead people."

I looked back to Lexi. "Let's go in."

Lexi made a face.

"Have you ever been in here?"

"Nope."

"You're scared of the dead, aren't you?"

"No, but I don't want to hang out with them."

"Come on. The cops will just drive up and down the street if they're looking for us. They'll never check out the graveyard. Besides, if they do there are lots of places for us to hide." I needed a little time to work out how I could stop Jon from leaving town —and also how I could break into his house. But I wasn't sharing that with Lexi. I waved her forward. "Come on."

We weren't the only ones visiting the dearly departed. There were people in little pockets everywhere, a few of them tourists like us, but I am sure some of them were the family of the dead. Walking down the main road we passed one such group having a picnic. Sitting on folding chairs with their lunch spread out on a stone coffin, they seemed to be enjoying their day.

"Creepy," Lexi murmured, looking at them sideways as if they were flesh eating cannibals. "You'd think they'd be leaving town or at least preparing for the storm."

"But maybe that's just what they're doing," I said. "Saying goodbye before they leave. It could all be changed when they come back." We'd both lived in Florida our whole lives and knew what a hurricane could do. Some people who leave ahead of a storm never return because there is nothing to come back to.

All the monuments seemed peculiar to me but the oddest one was a miniature red brick castle, about ten feet square and ten feet high with turrets at the corners, and with all of its arched windows bricked up to keep the dead in. The openings probably had always been sealed since the dead don't need to see out, so why go to the trouble of putting them there in the first place? Lexi nodded toward a giant finger of charcoal granite pointing up into the sky next to the brick castle. "Look at that. Those dearly departed are giving God the finger."

Some of the concrete coffins were piled on top of each other to save space, creating high rises of death. One such tower was five boxes high and five coffins wide. "Do you think it's all one family?" I asked as we walked by. Lexi didn't answer. She was still looking over her shoulder, probably searching for police – or maybe zombies. I wasn't worried about zombies or the cops; I was just waiting until I could go back to Jon's.

112

Older sections were almost derelict, monuments tilted and crumbling, graves that had sunk out of sight in the sandy soil. Wrought iron railings and brick walls surrounded blocks where families had their own little areas — just like the private family graveyard where I'd buried Clay.

You couldn't see much of the center of the cemetery from the street. What wasn't blocked by monuments was hidden by a forty-foot high gumbo limbo tree. With its peeling red bark, Floridians call it the sunburn tree or, more often, the tourist tree. Angels, Greek statues as tall as me, and concrete bunkers: was this a waking nightmare or a refuge? A seven-foot iron fence surrounded it all. I pointed to a deep depression. "Maybe this body has been dug up and moved. I had an uncle, Uncle Chubb, who was buried three times in a little family dispute."

"Just one more reason your family is so special."

"Gotta love those crazy people. They kept me entertained."

We paused in the shade of a geiger tree, heavy with clusters of frilled orange flowers. The tree hummed with bees.

"Speaking of crazy, you're in control again, aren't you? You weren't back at Jon's, but the wheels are turning now."

"Yup." It was true. The first horror of the situation was wearing off and my brain was starting to function. I was making lists of possibilities.

"What's the plan? I know you've got one."

"I've been thinking it through. Like you, I think Dix was on the bar all night, but the last part of the evening is a bit fuzzy for me. He may have taken a break and gone outside, met Marley, and done something to make her disappear."

"Like what?"

"Hit her on the head and stashed her in the trunk of his car. It would only take a couple of minutes."

"Why would he do that?"

"Why would anyone take Marley? Do you have security cameras outside?"

"Front and back. I want to know if someone is selling supplies, like steaks and ribs, out the back door."

"Will you check the cameras and see if there is any sign of Marley?"

"Sure."

"And e-mail your staff and tell them Marley is missing. See if anyone saw her after she left. I'll check out the place where Jon said they went for coffee." A gecko sat on a tombstone beside the path. His throat pulsed red, trying to attract a mate. Even among the dead, life goes on.

"You should spend more time in cemeteries. It sure smartens you up. Do you think the cops are still looking for us?"

"I don't know that they ever were."

"He called them. I'm sure of that. I saw him call."

"He could have been calling anyone." I stepped into the shade of the tree while she surveyed what she could still see of the street. At my feet was a pile of crumbled concrete. Salt air had taken its toll and now the roots of the tree were eating into what remained of the concrete. I had a sudden tingle of dread at the thought of the concrete giving away completely, of plunging down into a grave with the bones. A breeze sent a soft red flower brushing against my face. I batted it away, too aware of what its roots were feeding on. I said, "Let's get out of here."

Lexi pointed off to her right. "We should go through the cemetery and come out the other side."

"We'll be further from the scooter and it's too damn hot for a walk." I headed for the exit we'd come in, not caring if Lexi was following me.

When we got to the scooter I said, "Go by his house."

She made a wide and very unsteady U-turn. We paused in front of Jon's house. There was no sign of police. "He faked us out." The good news was that his vehicle was still in the drive.

"Stop," I said. The scooter double parked beside an Audi with a New York license. I slid off the seat and hustled to Jon's SUV with Lexi hissing, "Sherri," behind me. Marley was nowhere to be seen in Jon's vehicle.

"What now?" Lexi asked when I climbed on behind her.

"Well, you could knock on the door and keep him busy while I climb in the back window."

"Not going to happen."

"You want to go through the window while I keep him busy?"

"That's not going to happen either."

"Disappointing. Would Jon know many people in Key West?"

"Probably. He plays here every year."

"Let's check out Jon's story about going to the restaurant with Marley."

"Okay, but promise…"

"What?"

"Just take it easy."

"When I woke up this morning and saw Marley's door closed I was glad she was still sleeping, glad she wasn't there to tell me what a disaster I was. Now I'm saying, "Please God, bring her back. Don't let this happen. Please." Just talking about it was doing me in. "If there's any chance I can find her I'm going to take it."

Lexi nodded. "And I'm going to help you, but I would just rather not get arrested doing it. A girl like me would be a bit too popular in prison."

"Understood. I'll behave. The restaurant first and then you can check the tapes at the Rawhide, while I talk to some pedicab drivers." There was another thing I had to do, but I wasn't going to mention it to Lexi.

Chapter 17

At the Il Paradiso the first guy we talked to remembered Jon and pointed to another waiter. "Geo will help you. He served Elvis."

We wove our way through tables that were tightly packed together but mostly without customers, to where Geo was filling a salad bowl and mixing ingredients for the dressing. I told him why we were there and then I scrolled through the pictures on my phone. I held out the picture I'd taken the night before. "This is Marley."

"Pretty girl."

"Was she here with Elvis last night?"

"Yeah, that's the girl who was in with him." He handed the phone back to me and picked up the salad and the cheese grater. "She was wearing a hat but I'm sure it was her." He went off to deliver the salad.

"Marley hates hats," I told Lexi. "She refused to be maid of honor at my wedding if she had to wear a hat."

"Women do strange things for love."

"Maybe the hat was to hide beneath. We should have asked him what color her hair was." We waited. A waiter passed us carrying a huge tray on his shoulder. The smell of marinara sauce reminded me I hadn't eaten. Geo came back and scowled when he saw us still there. Before he could brush us off I asked, "Did she have red hair?"

"Couldn't actually tell you about the hair." He frowned. "Her hair was pulled back and tucked under the hat." He tilted his head sideways, remembering. "Except..." His face tensed with concentration. "Somehow, I would have guessed it was darker, auburn even, but not red." His fingers stroked imaginary tendrils at the side of his face. "There were wisps escaping." He shrugged. "Who knows? It was just my impression." He was already moving away.

I put a hand on his arm to stop him. "How did they seem?"

"What do you mean?"

"Well, were they acting like lovers or... whatever?"

"Didn't look like any love story to me." A hint of a smile. "She was really jumpy. I came up behind her and she nearly shot out of her chair. She glanced up at me quick and then looked down, kept her head down most of the night and didn't say a word to me. Hardly touched her tiramisu, couldn't wait to be out of here. I'd say she wasn't that into him." He thought about it a moment and raised his forefinger, pleased to have remembered. "Wait, yeah, he called her Marley, I remember now."

"And did it seem like they had just met?"

He tilted his head to the side, considering it. "They sat close together and talked a lot, not like lovers, but I would have said they knew each other really well. Didn't seem like they were really enjoying themselves and the guy kept watching the door."

"Like they were waiting for someone?"

"No idea. Look I'm not going to have to swear to any of this in court, am I? I'm just pretty much telling you my impressions, and it's not like I know any of it's true."

"She's missing and I'm just trying to find her. That's all I want, just to find her."

"That's a bummer, but I can't tell you anything more about them." He nodded toward the kitchen. "My order's up. Sorry I can't help more." He hustled to pick up the two plates waiting under heating lamps.

"That isn't much, except it says Jon was telling the truth. He was here with Marley." Lexi glanced around as if she'd just noticed we were in a restaurant. "Let's get a coffee."

"The woman with Jon last night wasn't Marley."

"How can you be so sure?"

"The hat, and then there's the way she acted. Marley isn't quiet and she isn't nervous." Elation grew in me with the certainty of my words. "It was someone who looked like her. Jon said he knew someone who looked like Marley. That's why he was so excited when he saw her."

"You can't be sure it wasn't Marley."

"Does it sound like Marley to you? She never shuts up and would be asking the waiter a million questions about the food even if all she was going to order was dessert. Let's see if
119

anyone saw them leave. We need to know if they got a pedicab the way Jon said. How many of those bicycle cabs are there?"

"I don't know… dozens or even hundreds. And they're going night and day. We need the police. We'll never get through them all."

Geo was hustling by with an order. I raised my arm, blocking his way. "Do you want a menu?" he asked, turning sideways to edge past me, a plate in each hand.

"Did you see Jon leave?" I asked.

"Hold on a second." He didn't even try to hide his annoyance as he went off to deliver the food while I simmered with frustration. How could everything go on as if nothing had happened, as if the world hadn't fallen into a black hole?

Geo came back and I asked again if he'd seen them leave. "They got in a pedicab." It was just as Jon had told us. Each part of his story was proving to be true, but only if the person in the restaurant was actually Marley.

Geo was smiling. Why was he smiling? Before I could ask he'd hurried off to pick up more orders.

I followed him. "Why did you think Jon taking a pedicab was funny?"

"It was who was driving the cab that was funny." He smiled again.

"And that was?"

"The angel," he said, and then he was gone.

"Angel? What the hell is he talking about?"

120

Lexi shook her head. "I don't know. We need help."

"I know a cop."

"In Key West?"

"Yeah."

"You're kidding?"

"Nope and I'm pretty sure I know where to find her. On Jackson Street. I saw her there today. Let's go down there."

She frowned. "I'm only going along with this so that you don't do something really stupid."

I pounded on the weathered red door that I'd seen Tanya entering. It took a while for her to open it, but it didn't take her long to tell me to get lost.

I told her about Marley's disappearance and the look-alike woman Jon was with the night before. "I'm sure it wasn't Marley."

"Maybe he bought her a hat so she wore it." She ruffled her bedhead hair standing up at odd angles.

"Why would he do that?" I asked.

"Haven't a clue but I saw their dance. Anything is possible after that." The door closed a little more.

"I need your help to get the police looking for her." I wedged myself into the opening. "If she isn't with Jon, where is she?"

"Again, I have no idea nor do I care, but I'm sure she'll be back soon. Go enjoy your day."

She tried to push me out the door but I wasn't moving. "We need to find her. You have to help."

"Not me," Tanya said. "I'm going to do my laundry and catch up on e-mails."

"Aren't you supposed to uphold the law and help people?"

"Oh, I'm doing that. I didn't shoot you, haven't hurt you in any way, have I? Tomorrow, if Marley doesn't show up, go back to the station and make a formal missing person's report. That's the best I can do."

"You might want to reconsider that decision."

Her eyes narrowed. Her lips locked in a hard line. "Why would I do that?"

I smiled. "Here's the deal. You help me find Marley and I won't tell Father Pat that you're a cop, the cop that's going to do him for drug dealing."

She opened her mouth to express her deepest feelings about me and then thought better of it. She clamped it shut. Her jaw worked. "Fine," she said at last. "What do you want?"

"I don't want Jon to leave Key West."

"I can't stop him."

"If you don't, I will."

"Threatening people is no way to get my help."

"Can you at least hurry the process up— get the Key West cops to start looking for her?"

She frowned. "I'll see what I can do. In the meantime, you should leave Key West before Alma arrives."

"Leaving as soon as I find Marley." I gave her my cell number. "I expect to hear from you." The door slammed in my face.

Chapter 18

From the back of the scooter, I saw that a piece of the puzzle had suddenly solved itself. I pounded on Lexi's shoulder and said, "There, over there," while pointing to an angel driving a pedicab. We followed her for half a block and then pulled in behind her as her passengers got down. I quickly scrambled onto the seat they had vacated.

"Where to?" she said, and gave me the world's biggest grin.

"I want to ask you some questions."

"Ask while I pedal."

"Okay, take me down to the beach."

"Good," she said. "I want to be on Duval Street at four o'clock. Every day I wave to my mother on the web-cam so she knows I'm still alive. She thinks the United States is very dangerous." She pedaled off like crazy, zigging and zagging through traffic with no regard for life or limb, waving to other pedicab drivers along the way and calling insults to others. As she pedaled, we talked. Giselle, a student on school holiday from university in Argentina, had caught the spirit of Key West. Half of her head was shaved and she was festooned with multiple piercings, including a silver stud in her tongue. With a big grin and almond eyes, she cycled passengers around town while wearing angel wings. She was a maniac on wheels.

"I know why you're wearing wings," I called to her. "You're practicing for your immediate future." I held onto the edge of the seat. "No point in getting to the web-cam in an ambulance. Your momma won't know it's you inside."

Nothing slowed the mad woman down.

When we got to where the camera was she raised her hand and waved wildly. I did too so Mama would know her daughter was still alive and living in Key West, driving friendly women around town.

Duval Street was shoulder to shoulder with tourists going in and out of the open doors of shops and bars. In cargo shorts, with multiple button-down pockets to protect their stuff and t-shirts proclaiming what they loved, Grandpa and Grandma were enjoying the show and delaying their evacuation until the last minute. It was all color and action and the approaching storm just added to the air of excitement.

Now that Giselle had reassured her mother she was fine, she leaned forward on the handlebars and took it easy, pedaling at the rate of a normal human being. "Pull over," I told her. I took out my phone and showed her the picture of Marley. "Did you pick up this woman, and a man dressed like Elvis, outside the Il Paradiso restaurant last night."

She looked at the picture and said, "I'm not sure it was this woman but I definitely remember Elvis." The big grin flashed across her face again.

"Where did you take them?"

"To Rude George's. He went inside and then she went somewhere else."

On the edge of the seat already, I leaned forward. My nails bit into my palms. "Where did you take her?"

"Why?"

"She's my best friend and she's missing. No one has seen her since last night and the police won't do anything until she's been gone seventy-two hours and no one…" I took a deep breath.

Giselle frowned. "Is she really missing?"

I nodded my head. "Since yesterday."

She stepped down from the bike seat and stretched her back as she thought about it. The edge of her hair was fringed with dampness and her face was flushed. "I remember. She got out at the bodega." A Cuban grocery store, at least it was a place to start looking for the woman who resembled Marley.

I sat back in the rickshaw. "Take me there."

I paid Giselle to wait for me while I went inside the store. The bodega was packed with people and it was all I could do not to shout at people in front of me to get out of my way. What I wanted was far more important than the bottles of water and loaves of bread they were getting in for emergency supplies. Some of them would be planning to run, but others would ride out the storm in emergency shelters or even their homes. Not me.

126

Run far and run fast is my motto when dealing with hurricanes. There's just nothing to be gained by staying. As soon as I found Marley, we were gone.

I finally got to the front of the line and showed the picture of Marley to the ancient Hispanic clerk.

"Sure, I seen her in here." He smiled, showing me where his teeth were missing, and passed my phone back. "Pretty girl."

"Do you know where she lives?"

"Nope." He looked past me to the next person in line and nodded at them.

Outside, before the door had closed behind me, Giselle hollered, "Any luck?" I shook my head and walked up a block and then back. In one of these houses the woman who looked like Marley was hiding out. "Wait for me," I told Giselle and went back into the store to ask another question, but the clerk had nothing more to tell me. Going out I bumped into a woman reaching for the door as I pushed it open. "Oh..." I stopped in shock. I was looking at Marley. Only it wasn't Marley but some weird almost-her. About thirty-five she had a few years on Marl, and she was a couple of inches taller with dark auburn hair, but she could pass. "Hey," I said.

She saw my face and immediately knew she was in trouble, bolting even as I reached for her. I missed her but grabbed her earbuds and with them her I-pod. I ran after her with the I-pod dangling from my hand. I did track in high school but I didn't have a hope of catching her. Toned and in shape, this woman hadn't spent her last ten years drinking and smoking.

While she was faster than me, she wasn't faster than Giselle, who pedaled madly down the street after the doppelganger. A block ahead of me I saw Giselle stop and then turn to look over her shoulder at me and frantically wave.

"She went through that gate," Giselle said as I huffed up to her. She pointed at a wooden gate in a hedge. "I think she may have gone over the back fence to the next street. "I'll go around there and see if she comes out."

I went through the gate into the back yard of a private residence. There was no place to hide and no sign of the woman, but a wrought iron gate to the next property stood open. I went through it.

When I came out to the sidewalk, Giselle was waiting. We hadn't caught the almost-Marley. We spent the best part of an hour going around the block, checking out alleys and backyards. The woman was gone, and she'd stay hidden now that she knew we were after her.

Giselle pulled out her phone and said, "Give me that picture." I did and she said, "I'll watch out for and her I'll send it to the other drivers."

When she had done that, I asked, "Do you know where there's a hardware store?"

"Yup. There's one on Eaton Street."

"Take me there."

Chapter 19

What tools do you need to break into a house? I settled on a small pry bar, in case Jon shut and locked his windows, a pen light, and a can of wasp spray that promised it could project the spray as far as twenty feet. The warning label said it was hazardous if it got in someone's eyes, might even cause blindness. I added a hunting knife, in case he kept coming after I hit him with the wasp spray. In the hunting section I found a backpack, covered in camouflage, to carry all of it.

Back at Petra's house, Lexi leapt down the front steps to meet me. A brief flame of hope sprang to life at her eagerness, but my anticipation was quickly squelched by her words. "Did you find out anything?"

"No."

"I called the hospital again and I called the police." She didn't have to add that they had no good news. "I told them Jon was the last person to see Marley, well except for the pedicab driver. And I told him about Jon recognizing Marley but... It's really kind of useless, isn't it?" We both knew our calls would be put under the heading of 'hysterical female' and forgotten. Lexi said, "I asked the cop if Tanya had started an investigation. He pretended he didn't know her. Hard to say one way or another if she has started working on it, but I think it was news to him." The corners of her mouth turned down. "I don't think she is doing anything."

"I doubt the person answering the phones knows what the detectives are investigating." I sighed. "You're probably right, though, Tanya won't do anything. It was worth a try."

"I'll have a word with her the next time she comes in."

I was betting that conversation would get loud. It made me smile.

Upstairs, I stuck the I-pod on to my own charger. The screen said, "Hello Jodi Kidd." Now I knew who I was looking for, Jodi Kidd. Maybe, if I found Jodi I'd find Marley. But how did I find Jodi? Did I have enough to take to the police? "Dumb Ass." I'd made a mistake in not getting Tanya's phone number.

"What is it?" Lexi asked. She still wore the track pants that bagged at the knees and the seat. The woman who dressed to be noticed had disappeared, leaving behind a desperate woman committed to something beyond beauty. "Does it tell you anything?"

"Yeah, I found something. Or rather, I found someone, Jodi Kidd. Must be related to Jon, maybe sister or wife, and she looks exactly like Marley. When I ran into her it took me a few seconds to realize it wasn't Marley. It was a shock and I hesitated. That was a mistake. Jodi saw that I recognized her and took off. I should have stopped her."

"Don't waste time beating yourself up. What do we do now?"

"Giselle has Marley's picture and she has sent it to the other pedicab drivers. They'll be watching, but we need to speed things up." A new worry gripped me. "Maybe I scared them when I bumped into Jodi. I wasted two hours looking for her. They might run sooner than they planned. They may be halfway to Miami."

Lexi pulled off the baseball cap. "We can't do anything about that if they have."

It was true but it didn't make me feel any better. "And we concentrate on Jon, because we don't know where Jodi is."

"Do you think she has Marley?"

"It's possible. If I watch Jon, sooner or later he'll take me to Marley or Jodi."

I called Rude George's to see if Jon was still going to be working. An annoyed voice told me he'd just arrived and the show would start in about forty-five minutes. I thanked them sweetly and hung up. "I haven't scared them off. If he's going to do the show I have two hours before he will be back at the house again. Plenty of time for what I'm going to do."

Lexi watched me intently. "What are you planning?" Her eyes widened. "Don't do anything stupid, Sherri."

"I need to get back inside that house."

Lexi threw her hands in the air. "Are you crazy?" She didn't wait for me to answer before she started to list all the

131

reasons that I should give up on that idea. She ended with, "You can't help Marley if you're in jail."

"I have only this one chance to find Marley. He's packing. When he's gone, he's not coming back. It will be police business at that point."

Lexi had a long list why it was a bad idea. Finally, she said, "You certainly can't do it before dark."

"He might only do one show and then run."

She thought that over. "Not likely if he wants to appear innocent. What do you want me to do?"

"Watch the front for me. Let me know if he comes home."

"And how am I supposed to do that?" And then she answered her own question, "Oh, I'll call your cell, right?"

"Might not be the best idea. I'm going to shut my phone off." I took it out of my pocket. "I'm going to do it right now because if it rings at the wrong time..."

"Well, what do I do if he comes back, toot my horn?"

The horn on the scooter was a pitifully silly sound. I knew because Lexi used it incessantly to tell people she was approaching. I'd never hear it inside the house. "Did you see that Beemer next door to Jon's? I bet it has an alarm. No one pays any attention to car alarms. If he comes back, just try to open the door of any car on the street and the alarm will go off and I'll hear it. I'll get out of there fast."

"Me too, I'm not waiting for some irate homeowner to show up."

Now that we had a plan, Lexi started worrying about the Rawhide. "I'm leaving them shorthanded. I can't just not show up."

"There won't be many customers tonight. And we haven't got a huge amount of time here, Lexi."

"I know, but I have to at least drop off more fliers. Georgie's going to help get them out."

"Fliers?" Lexi worked for every charity in town. What in hell did she think was more important than Marley's life? Probably some big fund-raising event where she got to dress up and strut around. Anger ripped through me. I headed for the bathroom to get away from her. If I said anything, I'd say too much.

Waiting for Lexi to change her clothes gave me time to think. The police weren't going to help and Tanya seemed to have let me down. I was counting on Giselle and the bicycle cabbies to come through for me and find Jodi. There were more of them than there were police. After a day without good news, I was willing to clutch at any straw. Most of all, I needed to get back inside Jon's house. It was my only hope.

Lexi was going to drop me back near Wrecker's Lane, but first I wanted to go to Rude George's and check Jon's SUV again.

A block from the apartment Lexi pulled over and pointed to a flier stapled to a telephone pole. "Yay!" she cheered. "They've already started putting them up." The poster said, "Have you seen this woman?" Below was a picture of Marley. Underneath that, it said she was missing and needed to be found urgently. There was also a phone number, Lexi's cell.

Lexi turned her head to the side to speak to me. "There are two hundred of them. They're going up all over town. And Petra Bishop is down on Duval Street handing them out. We'll find Marley." The scooter pulled away from the curb.

I hugged her in gratitude and whispered, "Thank you."

"I had to do something," Lexi said. "And that was all I could think of."

I saw more posters on the way to Rude George's. Lexi had been smarter than me and had done something concrete while I was running around town chasing a ghost.

Chapter 20

38 hours before Hurricane Alma hits Key West

At night, Key West changes from picket fence and gingerbread, with Mom and Pop tourists, to a younger and raunchier crowd, but oh my, were they good to look at. Every other guy seemed to have a two-day beard and delightfully rumpled hair. And they all seemed to favor linen slacks with silk shirts like it was the Key West uniform.

A hurricane warning had been issued that afternoon, and up and down the Keys homes had already been boarded up and evacuated. But not here. The bars and restaurants were still open and doing a roaring business.

We cruised around the block until we saw Jon's vehicle. Lexi pulled up beside it. "I'll walk back from here, but would you mind hunting Tanya down? I didn't get her telephone number and there's something I want her to do."

"What?"

"I called Rude George's again while I was waiting for you and asked if Jon was still there. He is, but it seems we aren't the only ones looking for him. Someone else called. I want Tanya to watch Jon." I knew there was only a slim chance of Tanya co-operating but I was desperate. "See if he goes anywhere between sets."

"Are you crazy? She'll never do that."

"She will if you convince her we're going to blow her cover."

"How will I find her?"

"Call the police station and say you have information for her. Or find Father Pat."

She heaved a great sigh. "What about you?"

"I can handle this on my own."

The approaching storm hadn't made any impact on the temperature. It was still hot and so humid it was like walking through a steam room. Sweat dripped off me. I took the penlight out of my backpack and shone it inside Jon's SUV. There were more bins than there had been the last time I'd looked, and the pole of clothes stretched across the back now had garment bags hanging from it, but there was no sign of Marley. Time to get to Wrecker's Lane.

Ahead of me strutted a tall thin black woman. She stopped at a wooden pole and stapled up a sheet of paper with a picture of Marley.

"Why?"

The woman turned to face me. Bleached blond and heavily made up, her Adam's apple bobbed, but to me she was beautiful. "You all right, Sugar?" she asked.

Pointing at the poster, I asked again, "Why?"

"What do you mean, Sugar? Why what?"

136

"This is my friend, so I'm looking for her, but why are you?"

"Lexi. She's got us all printing off these things and nailing them up all over town." She grinned. "When Lexi says do something, you do it. Besides, if one of us went missing, Lexi would move heaven and earth to help us." She reached out a comforting hand and patted my arm. "Don't worry, Sugar, we're gonna to find your friend."

I nodded and said, "Thank you." It was all I had.

Sunset was over but people still jammed Mallory Square. Even with Alma due to arrive within thirty-six hours, the beach hadn't slowed down.

The evacuation might have started in other parts of town, but you couldn't tell from the party going on here. If anything, it was even crazier, with a last chance feeling in the air. The crowd buzzed with a crazy excitement while the wind drove huge waves, covered in white caps, onto the beach. In the lights from shore, I could see three madmen a hundred yards off shore, risking their lives by surfing the big waves.

I pushed my way into the crowd to cross the square. In front of me, people were packed together watching a fire eater. Cheers went up every time he shoved the torch down his throat. Somewhere nearby a Reggae band was playing. I made my way through the square realizing I'd make a mistake coming this way.

137

Coming toward me was a guy on a unicycle balancing a dozen hats on his head. A woman stepped backwards into his path. He turned quickly, wobbling crazily and almost falling. The hats piled on his head tumbled down and he grabbed at them while trying to get the unicycle under control. A top hat bounced off the woman in his way and she screamed. "Sorry, Love," the unicyclist said in an English accent as he retrieved his hats from the bystander who had picked them up.

The woman's partner, face bloated, shirt hanging out, and well on his way to being seriously drunk, started swearing and cursing the unicyclist.

"Leave it, Joe," the blonde said, tugging on his arm. Her worried eyes said this was an all too familiar situation.

"No, that asshole almost ran you down. And then he belts you with a piece of his junk." He was the kind of drunk who started looking for a fight long before he was even over the limit, a fight being his reason for drinking. "No," he said again. "I won't leave it."

"It wasn't his fault," said a guy in dreadlocks and sandals, trying to make peace. "Let's all just enjoy our evening."

"Mind your own business," the drunk said, jabbing a finger at the Rastafarian.

An older man broke through the edge of the crowd. "Your wife should look where she's going."

I tried to move away from the confrontation but the crowd had bunched up behind me, wanting to see this new entertainment.

"Bloody hippies," the drunk growled, making a grand gesture with a plastic cup of beer. The bitter smelling liquid splashed down my shirt.

There was more yelling. As acid flowed up my throat, I pushed through the surrounding bodies. The heat coming off the sidewalk and the smell of the beer coming off my shirt made me lightheaded. Behind me fireworks lit up the sky. I stumbled off to Wreckers Lane.

At the first house on Wrecker's Lane, a light burned at the back. I slipped along, staying close to the vines that clung to the fences, past the hedge of the second house, trying to stay unseen, and hidden in the shadows. If anything went wrong, I didn't want anyone to remember me. The alley was so overgrown that the full moon had no influence on the visibility.

The light went out on the first house as I made my way along the back lane, barely able to make out the houses and wondering what I was stepping in. Staying close to the board fences walling off each property, I moved around the sliver of light shining on the edge of the pathway from what I thought was the back of the third house. The sweat slipping down my spine wasn't just from the heat. Should I risk using my penlight or would it attract attention? It wasn't worth the risk. I counted the

139

houses past the big Cyprus hedge at the corner to make sure I had the right place. Breaking into the wrong house wasn't part of my plan, but then I've done dumber things.

I reached out for the fence and bumped into something big and bulky. I felt along it. It was a mattress. There had been one leaning up against the fence just outside Jon's house. This was the place. The gate should be just a few feet past this. The house was in complete darkness. Only the ragged outline of the trees it sheltered under and the straight line of the roof were visible in the faint light. The broken down wooden gate squeaked. I froze. Scuttle back or move forward? I ran for the dark shadow of a palm, stepping on a dead frond and stumbling. As I stood still and gathered my courage, something soft glided across my legs. I jumped away from the cat as if it were fire. "Damn thing," I hissed aloud, before I could stop myself. A yowl went up.

Nearby someone laughed in the dark. I raised my head to see if anyone was coming down the alley. I couldn't tell, but I moved deeper under the tree and waited. From the street in front of the house came the sound of a car door slamming. I hoped Jon hadn't come back early but no lights came on in the house.

No lights, no sounds. Surely the house was empty, and I was alone with my overactive imagination.

I'd been hunkered down in this overgrown garden for long enough. Time to make things happen. I had under an hour — less if Jon decided to cut his performance short. Fear kept me
140

crouching there. Much easier to do something in the heat of the moment than to plan it and wait for it to happen. I began to count, promising myself when I reached twenty I'd move. And then I counted to twenty again.

Breathe. No denying I was afraid, but there was something I was even more scared of – losing Marley. In my day-to-day life, she was pretty much the only thing that was still keeping my feet on the ground. Without her... well, let's just say it wouldn't be pretty.

Move or go home. I stood. I'd crouched there so long my legs cramped. Shaking them out, I got the blood flowing again. Had Jon closed the window in the spare room? *Don't worry about that until it happens.* Bent low, I slipped to the open window.

I put the chair under the window and carefully climbed up. The screen fell in on my first push. I waited, holding my breath and listening hard. No one came. I pulled myself up on the sill, hung on my belly for a minute, then tilted forward and fell down the wall into the bedroom. I scuttled into the shadow of the bed, away from the view of anyone coming into the room. There were no squeaking floorboards to say someone was creeping toward me. I turned on the penlight and searched under the bed. I wasn't going to leave anything unchecked this time. If Marley was in this house I would find her.

The closet contained a vacuum. There was nowhere else to look in the ten by twelve room. Easing the door open, I slipped into the hall. Across the hall and into the bathroom, the penlight shone on creeping damp, missing tiles, and grunge. There was no shower curtain because there was only a tub with a weird spray attachment. But things had changed in here since this morning. The small counter around the sink had overflowed with tubes, half empty and screwed up, lotion bottles with the tops off and hair everywhere, but now only the black strands of Jon's hair remained. I backed out.

The main bedroom, across the width of the house at the end, was sparsely furnished with few places to hide anything. I checked them all quickly. The only things under the unmade bed were dust and a ragged stack of tattered porn magazines. The closet was empty. A suitcase, half filled, was on the bed with a pile of clothes beside it.

On the floor was plastic bin of personal junk. I riffled through the box looking for answers. A Frisbee, a clock radio, bills for a post office box in Atlanta Georgia, nothing to help me find Marley. I picked up a picture frame tucked into the side. When I turned it over, Marley smiled up at me. She was dressed in jeans and a t-shirt and was posing on a sail boat. I looked closer. Was it really Marley? I couldn't tell. I dug through the box and found another picture. This time I knew it was Jodi. She was dressed as a show girl in an ad for a hotel in Vegas. On the back in blue ink it said, "How do you like me now, Bro?" One question was answered. Jodi was Jon's sister. I took a Bank of

America letter with the Atlanta postal address, and the Vegas picture of Jodi, and put them in my backpack.

I searched the kitchen quickly, even checking under the sink and opening every cupboard door. Not worrying about closing them, not trying to hide the fact that I'd been there. Fear should be making me cautious but instead my need to find something before Jon got back was overpowering my ability to reason. More cupboards and more nothing! The clock on the kitchen wall told me I had less than fifteen minutes until the end of Jon's set.

In the living room, I looked around. There was no place to hide an adult among the oversized blue ceramic lamps, the artificial wood end-tables and the brown nubby couch. My mother, Ruth Ann, would call it Swedish modern but it hadn't been modern for fifty years at least. A television sat opposite the couch. Above it a red ceramic matador fought a charging bull. The room smelled of the stale cigarettes that spilled out of overflowing ashtrays.

Lights swept across the wall of the living room from a vehicle turning into the drive. I'd run out of time.

Chapter 21

I pushed off the window ledge and hit the edge of the chair, knocking it over. I fell back against the house. The sound resonated out into the night. No longer worried about noise or tripping over something, I ran across the dark yard.

Without light, it was hard to find the gate. Panic was building in me. *Slow down and take a deep breath. No one is coming after you.* It was true. But about now Jon would realize his house had been searched. He'd see the screen on the floor of the open window. Hard to guess how he might react. Would he follow me out the window or just finish packing and get away?

Fighting panic and a desire to belt down the lane, I stayed close to the fence, as deep in the shadows as I could get, waiting and listening. Jon would guess his intruder would go down the lane and might wait there for me.

At the mouth of the alley, I huddled in the shadows, waiting. Even though a strong breeze was blowing, it was still about eighty degrees out and the dark jeans and jacket I was wearing were making me sweat — or maybe it was fear. I took off the jacket and stuffed it in the backpack and then I stepped out of the alley. I was alone.

Going into that house had been for nothing – a useless risk. Marley was still gone and I was no closer to knowing why. But if I hadn't taken it... How do you live with the memory of the things you didn't do? For me it might turn out to be just as bad as living with my mistakes.

Was there anything else I could try? I still had no idea where Marley was. The possibility that she might be somewhere close, that I might walk right by her and not even know she was there, was unbearable. Somehow, I felt I should be able to feel her presence, to sense telepathically where she was if only I concentrated hard enough. But it wasn't happening.

I hadn't seen anything to prove that Marley had even been in the house. Was there a place Jon could hide her that I hadn't found? Under the floor? I started to picture a body wrapped in black trash bags. *Don't go there. Marley isn't a body.* I couldn't, and wouldn't, think that.

My steps slowed. In my mind, I walked through the house again, room by room, searching for some clue I'd missed. But there was still nothing. What about the garden, could she be hidden deep in those shadows? Not likely, because I'd had a good look over the gate earlier, and there was no shed or anything like it to hide a person in. What had I missed? *You'll find her. Don't even think of anything else. Hang on and believe. Keep trying.* But I was running out of time and ideas. I trudged along on my way back to the Rawhide, trying to find answers to questions.

Jon was leaving Key West. Would he be taking Marley with him? Why hadn't he run before? If taking her off island was what he wanted, you'd think he'd be on the road as soon as he accomplished it. Why was he still here? Either he didn't want to look suspicious, wanted to alibi himself, or he had to do something before he ran. Not for a minute did I consider that he was leaving ahead of the hurricane like everyone else.

Where was Jodi? And did she have Marley? It seemed the most likely possibility now.

How long since I left the house? Twenty minutes? He might be gone already.

I whirled around and started walking back as fast as I could.

The black SUV was in the driveway and blocked in by a light-colored sedan parked behind it. Did two vehicles mean Jodi was there? Was there something they needed to do before they left?

I took out the penlight and shone it inside the cargo area of the SUV. Nothing had been added since I checked earlier. He hadn't picked up anything from Rude George's or on the way home. At least nothing that would hold Marley. There wasn't anything on the floor but fast food containers and a pair of trainers, the same as before. The front seat was empty.

"Shit."

I went to the sedan. The light picked out the interior. No Marley on the front seat or in the back. In fact, there wasn't even a scrap of paper, the opposite of Jon's mess. That only left the trunk. I had the crowbar. Would an alarm go off when I pried open the trunk? *And do I care?* If they came out of the house I'd be happy to see them and say hello with the working end of the iron bar.

Still, how exactly do you jimmy open the trunk of a car? At a time like this, I could really use my old man's advice. The one thing Tully Jenkins excelled at was breaking into things and causing mayhem. I jammed the lever in just below the lock. Turned out that popping the trunk wasn't all that hard. No alarm went off. That was the good news. The bad news was the trunk was empty, as pristine as though it had never been used. I slammed the lid closed. It sprang open. I tried several more times with the same result.

I switched off the penlight and stood there trying to decide where to look next. The house had no basement and no garage. I had to come to terms with a hard truth: wherever Marley was, she wasn't here.

Chapter 22

I wanted to know who was inside the house and I wanted to hear what they were saying. With darkness, the wind had come up. Now it was whipping debris around, wailing and whining like some evil interloper. There was no way to hear anything from outside. Besides, if they were in Jon's room the old-fashioned air conditioner, used to supplement a dying system, filled the window and gave them perfect protection from eavesdropping.

If I went back inside I could hear everything. I considered it. How dumb was that idea on a scale of one to ten? About an eleven. But this was my last chance. Anger won out over terror. But first I needed to slow him down when they left the house. I hunkered down by the rear tire of Jon's SUV, removed the cap on the valve and rammed in the corner of the crowbar. Then I called Lexi. When they did leave, we would need to follow them and hope they led us to Marley. Lexi's phone was turned off. I was staggered by the betrayal. So much for friendship. I was on my own.

I slipped around the house, going past the kitchen door to the back. Water was running. Lots of it. I knew what it was. There was an outdoor shower smack in front of me and someone was in there. Lots of Florida homes still have these showers, especially older houses like this one. Built before every house had air conditioning, these exterior showers keep the heat and the steam out of the house and prevent mold. Some people swear by them and can't understand why anyone would want to shower indoors. Here was something I'd missed and it explained why Jon's bathroom only had a tub. It was comforting to know he wasn't worried about time, freshening up after work before he made a run for it. Or maybe he was setting himself up for an all-night drive that would put him in North Carolina or Alabama by this time tomorrow. By the time the seventy-two hours had passed and the cops finally put Marley on a missing persons list and got interested enough to question him, Jon could be anywhere. And by then Alma would have arrived. It might be days or even weeks before the Key West police started looking for her.

I listened to the shower. Jodi was the only one inside the house. She may be faster than me but I was betting I was a whole lot meaner. I got out the wasp spray, hoping she didn't carry anything more lethal. Not that I would never need a weapon because they weren't going to know I was there, were they?

The bedroom was still in darkness. I righted the chair and placed it under the window. It tilted as I climbed onto it. I held onto the sill to balance myself and then hefted my body up on the ridge of the dark window. A light was on in the hall. If the sedan belonged to Jodi, she'd be in the living room. Not even the most devoted sister would do his packing.

Wasp spray in hand, I tilted forward like a great blob of plasma from a horror movie, half in and half out of the window, before sliding down the wall and falling on the window screen. There wasn't much noise, but there was enough to alarm me and keep me fixed at the window ready to bolt. I crept to the door where I could hear anything that might be said when Jon came in.

But Jon wasn't in the shower. He was on the floor in the hall with a black-handled knife protruding out of his body.

Chapter 23

I froze, staring at him. "Jon?" The whisper was so soft that even if he weren't dead he wouldn't have heard. I stepped into the hall, not quite believing he was beyond help. There was so much blood. I didn't know there could be so much in one human being. Blood had spurted up the wall and over the faded picture of a waterfall. A spray of blood had splattered in an arc across the ceiling. It was as if an excited teenager had shaken a quart of soda and let it spray the room. And in the gore, there were signs that Jon been trying to get to his feet right to the end. Blood was smeared where his legs had bicycled back and forth, trying to get purchase. It hadn't worked, and he was never going to get to his feet again.

The aluminum door squeaked open. Voices. Not Jodi. Men's voices. A man stepped into the entrance to the hall, followed by a naked man toweling himself off.

I ran for the window. No need to be quiet anymore. I heard a curse and pounding feet, coming for me. Out the window, I hit the ground hard. And then there were more curses mingled with the rattle of the chair that my pursuer had landed on.

I knew the backyard and he didn't. A small advantage. Also, I was running for my life. Out the gate and down the alley. I could feel his nearness, waited for a hand to grab me. At the end of the alley, I was sure fingertips grazed my hair. But I'm practiced at dodging hands.

I didn't slow down to check traffic, didn't pause for the horn that blew. He did. I made it across the street. I ran with no clear thought, footsteps pounding on the sidewalk behind me.

I came to the hole under the fence. I reacted without thinking, falling flat and squirming under the fence.

On my feet, I risked glancing back. The guy was steroid huge and still coming. Maybe he wouldn't be able to get under the fence — or I could go back and shoot him with the wasp spray while he tried. But it was no longer in my hand.

Go. I raced away into the dark. The full moon that was bringing in the high tides was the only light, but there was enough for me to avoid crashing into tombstones — and enough for him to find me.

Who else used that hollow under the fence to access the graveyard? *Don't think about that,* my little voice warned. But how do you stop your fears? Guys hanging out here on the dead grounds were not going to be my friends. *Neither is the guy behind you.*

A primitive survival instinct took over, firing orders, telling me not to go down the straight alley of tombs, but to zig and zag. My advantage might be agility. The killer was heavy but he had muscle and he had speed. Something heavy toppled from one of the crypts behind me. I shot around a tall brick structure, a miniature castle without windows, bolted past two

152

more rows of tombs, and then lunged right toward a huge tree I could hide beneath. I tripped on a root. The air that was knocked out of me came with a startled yelp. Back on my feet, trying to move but something held me. He'd captured the back pack. My shoulders went back and I shucked it off. Catapulting forward, I ran over graves, dodged behind tombs and under branches. I had no idea if he was still chasing me. I just ran for my life.

I was no longer trying to be quiet. The goal here was to stay alive and that meant keeping ahead of him. In the moonlight, the giant gumbo limbo tree, dancing in the growing wind, stood out against the moon. I headed for it, slipped in close, and leaned back against its comforting surface, needing time to get my breath back.

Squatting down, making myself as invisible as possible, I gulped for air, while my fingers searched the ground for something to defend myself with. I'd lost my knife with the backpack. *Hit him hard, if not to finish him off, at least to slow him down.* My frantic hands found nothing, not a stick or a stone or a hunk of concrete. I searched further from the base of the tree. And then from beside me rose a body, like it was rising from a grave. Maybe it was. It was only a shape…and a smell. A bad smell. A smell of rot and decay.

The apparition swore. A jumble of muttered curses, evil incantations, and the foulest language ever heard from the dead. Undead or just a homeless man sleeping rough, it didn't matter, because the shadowy shape of another man came around the end of a monument.

I saw the club he held in his raised hand. The specter I'd disturbed reacted like a trained commando, moving forward to engage his new enemy.

I ran. Behind me, grunts and groans and curses and then there was a great crash. Not a body falling, but something heavier like maybe they'd toppled a shrine. I heard a shout.

Deeper into the grounds, I was moving away from my escape route. *Will I be able to find it again?* There was a bigger fear. I was sure there were more men out here in this dead zone that I didn't want to meet. *Don't think about that.* But how?

Hiding was all that made sense. In front of me was a huge block of tombs, probably ten feet by ten feet. The overlapping edges of the individual sarcophagi might make it possible to climb to the top, providing the rotting concrete didn't crumble under me. Once on top, I could hide out until daylight. A night in a cemetery wasn't anyone's idea of a good time but neither was being clubbed to death. I was almost desperate enough to try it. Almost. *There's nothing to say he'll give up, won't just be there waiting when I raise my head in the morning.* I searched for signs of motion around me. Branches thrashed in the wind. Bushes moved. I looked away.

If I worked my way to the outside, to the fence, I might find another escape route. The guys living here would have more than one way in. *Good luck with that.* The exit wouldn't be obvious. Would there be a marker they could find in the dark? Slowly walking along the six-foot high fence would make me stand out in the light of passing cars. An easy target.

So, what's it going to be? that annoying little voice in my head asked. *Crawling under the fence or hiding?* I had no answer.

Chapter 24

I slipped down in the deep shadow of a monument. How far had I come into the warren of concrete crypts? Doing nothing seemed a good idea. At least it was better than doing the wrong thing. Huddling there, I realized I could smell lilies. My hands searched the ground around me, hunting for them. At the base of the giant finger of granite, my fingers closed on a tall slender vase. I took out the flowers, poured the water on the ground, and held it just below its flared top, ready to beat the daylights out of anyone who came near me.

Time passed. Leaves chattered and branches knocked in the swelling wind. The noise was beginning to sound like dozens of skeletons moving in on me. A graveyard at night does things to the imagination.

Suddenly, somewhere in the dark beyond the fence, I heard the irritating toot of Lexi's tiny horn. To me it sounded like the angel Gabriel calling me home. But how could I get to it? I eased around the monument to see where the sound had come from and saw the headlight of her scooter, shining like a beacon. She was parked on the street not fifty yards away, waiting. There was a stone tomb a few feet from the fence. Could I use it to get over the barrier? As I weighed the possibilities, Lexi drove slowly away. I watched until her headlight was out of sight.

Seconds later a car coasted slowly down the street. I knew that sedan. Its trunk was still open. "Careful, Lexi," I whispered. She didn't know what danger she was in and there was no way to warn her.

The fighters had gone silent. No swearing or yelling. Hopefully they'd killed each other, but it was more likely they'd gone their separate ways and were now both out there hunting for me.

One thing was certain, Jon's murderer wouldn't give up looking for me now that I'd seen his face. *Get the hell out of Dodge.* No way he was going to let me live. *Get out of this graveyard and then get home.* That thought was quickly followed by another. *Not yet, not without Marley.*

Staying still was harder than moving, but I was disoriented. How far into the maze of tombstones had I come? Where was the crawl space below the iron railing that had been my entrance?

Creeping silently from the protection of one tomb to the next, hiding in the shadows and listening before I moved on, I worked my way back to where I thought I'd entered the grounds. Lexi drove by again, tooting her horn. At the very least someone was going to call the cops and report her. *Fine with me.* I'd kiss the ground the cop walked on and smile all the way to jail.

Suddenly, in the dim light, I recognized the outline of a monument. I knew where the opening was. Slowly, slowly, slipping from shadow to shadow, I worked my way back toward

157

the tiny entrance under the iron fence. But I stopped before I got there. I waited. *Where is he?* Would he guess that I'd try to go out the same way I came in? The longer I waited, the more likely he was to come back to this place.

The little headlight came around the corner and shone briefly toward me before it swung down the empty street. I shimmied under the fence and ran out into the street, waving my arms. The little pink motor bike fishtailed and stopped a foot from me.

I scrambled on the scooter, screaming "Go, go." I watched behind us to see if we were followed but the street was empty.

Lexi slowed and turned down Truman Ave. "Are you all right? What in hell happened? Why didn't you come back to the Rawhide?"

"I'll tell you at home." Crossing Duval, Lexi slowed nearly to a stop. Two guys, one wearing a black leather suit and white lizard boots, the other in tight jeans and a white muscle shirt, were dancing on the edge of the sidewalk to the music pounding out of Rude George's. I poked Lexi in the shoulder and said, "Dancing Queens." She circled wide around them, staying well out in the center of the street so there was no chance of sideswiping them or even disturbing them.

I laid my head on her shoulder. Fear chased recriminations in my mind. *Why didn't you use the crowbar to*

158

disable both vehicles and keep them at Jon's? All you had to do was call the cops and tell them... Tell them what? I lifted my head to consider that question. *Anything, you could have told them anything.* But I hadn't known Jon was dead. I just wanted to know what Jon and Jodi had been planning.

The energy that fear gives ebbed away. My adrenalin rush turned to shock. I laid my head down again on Lexi's shoulder to rest. I may have even slept.

"Jesus, I feel like a fool," Lexi said when she was parked at the side entrance to Petra Bishop's house. She'd changed into dark jeans, a black jersey and a black baseball cap that sported a big red rose. Even for a break-in a girl should wear a bit of glitz.

I was barely able to stand up so I didn't bother with conversation. A discussion for one never bothered Lexi so she carried on. "When Jon came home, I headed up to the house, trying to delay him and give you more time. Hell, I didn't know what I was going to do, I just wanted to distract Jon, give you a chance to get out of there if you were hiding inside, or help you if he caught you. I pretended I was there to see him." We walked slowly around to the front veranda. "I propositioned him. He blew me off — no pun intended. That guy is so straight..." She searched for a comparison and couldn't come up with one. "Well, he isn't interested in girls like me. How can I ever face him again?"

"Well, here's the good news." She opened the gate and I led the way up the brick walkway and collapsed onto the second step. "You won't ever have to see him again."

"Why?" She sat down beside me and draped her arm over my shoulder. "Is he leaving town?"

I leaned on her. "He's dead."

She jerked away from me. "Shit," she said. She held me at arm's length and stared at me. "I always knew that one day your temper..." She didn't finish.

"I didn't do it. There were two men there."

"Shit," she said again.

"Lexi, did you see anyone else at the house besides Jon?"

"Yeah. Just as he went in and shut the door, a car pulled up and blocked the drive. There were two men inside."

"Any idea who they were?"

"Nope. I didn't pay any attention. I just wanted to get out of there and find you." She canted her head to the side. "That's not quite true. I glanced at them when I went by the car. They had their heads down, ignoring me, but I don't think the driver was anyone I know."

But they'd know her anywhere. Everyone in Key West would probably recognize Lexi. A six-foot woman, tall, broad shouldered and wearing sequins, stood out. The killer just had to describe the woman he'd met on the sidewalk to any resident of the town and he'd be told, "Why, that's Lexi Divine, Darling." It

160

was a scary thought. If Jon's murderer thought Lexi could identify him, he'd come after her. She'd go ballistic when I told her and right now I had nothing left for the drama. I'd warn her in the morning.

We sat there in silence. Finally, Lexi asked, "Are we going to call the cops about Jon?"

I worked on it for a minute. It didn't take long to decide. "Nope."

"That seems cruel, just leaving him there."

"I want a little time."

"For what?"

"To find Marley. I thought if I followed Jon he'd lead me to Marley."

"If the police know that Jon is dead, won't they start looking for Marley? You told them he kidnapped her."

"Good point. Or maybe they'll spend all their time trying to prove I did it."

She gave me a hug and stood up. "Let's go upstairs and put this night behind us."

I didn't bother to tell her that I had to go back to the graveyard and look for my backpack. I wanted that picture, proof that there was someone who looked almost exactly like Marley. It would also prove that Marley's disappearance and Jon's murder were linked. Perhaps it would be enough to start them looking for Marley. It might also make them look at me as a murderer.

Tomorrow.   Nothing was happening tonight. I needed time and rest. Nothing could convince me to go back there in the dark. And tomorrow Lexi and I had to decide how we were going to ride out the storm. Time was slipping away and with it my options.

Chapter 25

Sunday, 17 hours before Hurricane Alma hits

It was barely daylight when that rooster began to crow. For once I was grateful to have him wake me. There were things I wanted to do without having to explain them to Lexi. I dressed quickly and silently left the house.

Wind pushed back at me when I opened the door, and ominous low clouds hung on the horizon. Alma was making her presence known, sooner than I had expected. It did not bode well for Key West if she came in early. Growing up in a mobile home, this was always the time that even my mother and the rest of the stragglers would flee. Our car would be packed to the ceiling and I'd kneel on the back seat to watch our tin box with its pink metal awnings, lowered now to protect the windows, till we made the turn onto the highway, sure we'd never see it again. Three times we'd left, and three times it had survived. The last time, though, the wind had ripped off the carport. Mom had never had the money to replace it. The long gash below the roof line had been tacked over with an angry strip of reclaimed metal. That patch had come to symbolize our lives. Hang on, cover it up, and endure.

As I walked down the steps, I thought of Marley. She'd be freaking out if she was watching the approaching storm. Her family was always the first to evacuate.

A long black cat leapt from the bushes at the bottom of the stairs. Startled, I yelped and jumped sideways. With a glare of disgust, the cat slunk deep into the tall ferns beneath the live oak. This got the long walk back to the cemetery off to a good start, set my feet moving quickly. And the gusting wind helped carry me down the street as I bounced from one disaster to another in my head. Jon's death made Marley's situation even more perilous.

Why do you kill a man and then take a shower? The answer to that was easy. To get the blood off. Walking around dripping red would get you noticed. If he had killed one person there was nothing to stop him from killing again. If the murderer had Marley... *There's no advantage to going there.*

Why Marley? The question I'd always come back to now had an answer. Marley had been taken because she looked so much like Jodi Kidd. Jodi had been impersonating Marley at the restaurant, I was certain of that. Had Marley been substituted for Jodi somewhere else? I had to find Jodi. How could I do that?

And had she been talked into going willingly? Marley was the kind of person who always wanted to help others, just like that kid who would help the pedophile find his lost puppy. Her unsuspecting nature made dealing with a con artist problematic.

164

Now that Jon was dead the only person who could answer my questions was Jodi. *Find her and I'll find Marley. But where do I start?* I needed that picture of Jodi. Put that image side by side with Marley's and even the most jaded cop was going to take an interest. Add Jon's death to Marley's disappearance and they had to see there was something terribly wrong. But telling them how I knew about Jon's murder might complicate the situation.

The deserted streets had taken on an eerie feeling. Plywood had been fastened to the outside of windows to keep flying debris from shattering them when hurricane winds blew in. The sound of hammering said that a few people were still preparing for the coming storm but already on the side streets the town had an abandoned feeling.

The police were blocking cars from coming down the Keys. Cruise liners had been rerouted, the last of the tourists would leave today and most of the residents of Key West would go with them. It might be days or weeks before they could return. What people outside of Florida never realize is that it isn't the winds themselves that do the damage but the rains and flooding that come with the wind. The highest land on Key West is only eighteen feet above sea level. With a twenty-foot surge... When you lose your power, leaving no air conditioning, refrigeration, fresh water or flush toilets, it's just not as much fun as we pretend. I would be running for shelter as soon as I found

Marley. To do that, I had to find Jodi, but try as I might, I couldn't come up with one place to start looking.

The gates to the cemetery were still locked. I found the hollow under the fence. I had a good look around. It was Sunday morning sleepy, no one on the street, but that didn't mean no one was there. The memory of events from the night before had my nerves jumping and jiving. *Wish I had the wasp spray.* Nineteen acres, that's what Lexi said this iron fence surrounded. In here, I could get my throat slit and it would be days before anyone found me. Not a good thought and not helpful at all.

I got down on my belly and shimmied under the fence. Listening, all I could hear were birds and somewhere close the sound of a drill putting in screws. Checking about me for signs of life, I threaded my way through the monuments. I really had no idea of the path I'd taken last night. I worked my way back and forth, trying not to get impatient. Twenty minutes later I still hadn't found the backpack and, I decided, I wasn't going to. *Does it matter?* This thought was quickly followed by another. *That depends on who has it.* The killer knew I could identify him so he wasn't going to like me walking around. If he knew who I was, he'd come for me. Not a good thing. *Was there anything in the backpack that could identify me?* The answer came quickly. There was. I scrambled through my wallet looking for the receipt for my purchases but it wasn't there. I'd shoved it into the backpack with the rest of the stuff. Normally it wouldn't be a problem, but the computers at the hardware store had been down and the clerk had put through the transaction the old-fashioned way. The imprint of my card, with my name on it, was on the receipt.

Perhaps some homeless person had found the pack. *Yeah, and perhaps I'll be reincarnated as one of the rich and famous after he kills me. Something to look forward to.* I jogged back to the dip below the fence. I might not be the only one to have returned to the graveyard. I crouched down at the fence and glanced around, trying to identify a watcher. No one on the street, and nobody sitting in a parked car, at least not that I could see. Quickly, feeling vulnerable, I wiggled under the fence. I jumped up, ready to bolt, and brushed off my clothes. Checking again to see if anyone was watching, I walked away quickly.

I couldn't go straight back to the apartment if someone was following me. Veering left, I slipped in between two houses with the front windows boarded up, hoping there wasn't a big dog in the shade of the backyard. A short fence separated the tiny back lawn from the one on the next street. I was over it quickly. I came out between the houses onto an empty street. I used the same maneuver again between two houses on the other side of the street. This time I wasn't so lucky. An elderly man was sitting in the morning sun, taking time out from covering the last of his windows. "Good morning," I said, and quickly reversed. I had a good look up and down the street before leaving the shadows between the little cottages.

On the next block was a house with a For Sale sign on it. The windows had steel shutters over them and there was no car in the driveway. Whoever lived there was already gone. I glanced from side to side and then went up the shell drive. I needed to make some calls. My name could quickly be found on the internet. Anyone who searched for me would learn all about what had happened in Jacaranda, Florida. Then they only needed to call the restaurant and be told where I was staying in Key West. I had to stop that from happening.

The backyard had been emptied of everything that could fly around in the storm. I sat on the root of a banyan tree and accessed the answering machine at the restaurant. Sure enough, a man had left a message saying that he'd met me in Key West and was supposed to pick me up for a boat trip but had forgotten the address. Could someone please call him back and let him know where I was staying.

It wasn't all bad. I had his telephone number. But if he was smart enough to find me, he was probably smart enough to have a disposable phone. Surely there was some way I could use his cell to find him. The police could do it.

Experience told me that starting the conversation about how I'd come by the number would take more than ten minutes. It would go around and around, and then they would leave me waiting while they checked up on my story, and then they'd come back and start all over again. I could end up spending hours waiting just to give them a statement. After I found

168

Marley, or there was no place left to look, then they could take their time listening to what I had to say.

I called Gwen, the manager at the Sunset. She wasn't happy to hear from me. Working late at the restaurant, she'd expected her Sunday morning to have a bit of a late start. After she finished explaining this to me, she said she hadn't told anyone about Lexi, the Rawhide, or anything else that would help the killers find me. "Why would I?"

"Does anyone else know I'm staying with Lexi?"

"Not unless you've told them."

I hadn't. One good thing.

It was too early to call Giselle. Pedicab drivers would be night people too so I had to wait and trust that she'd get in touch with me if she had anything to tell me. If she hadn't called by noon I'd check in with her.

I had to go back to the apartment to face Lexi and tell her Jon's murderers might be coming for her. She was a memorable figure in Key West. Anyone might tell them where to find her.

Chapter 26

Petra was sweeping the sidewalk as I turned the corner. She stared intently at me. My footsteps faltered. She shook her head, just a fraction, and then turned around and swept back to her front gate. I pivoted and walked away.

I started jogging and was four blocks away before I pulled out my phone and called Lexi. "Where are you?" she asked.

I told her.

"The police just left, but they're sitting out front."

"What do they want with me?"

"Yesterday you were accusing Jon of kidnapping and telling Tanya you weren't going to let him leave Key West. Today he's dead. Of course, they want to speak to you."

"I don't want to talk to them yet. I can't find Marley if I'm sitting in the station. Besides, they already know everything I know about her disappearance."

"All right. Stay where you are. I'll come as soon as I can."

A half hour later a beat up old jeep pulled up beside me. Its front window was cracked and its scabby green paint showed metal. "Get in," Lexi said.

She checked the side mirror and pulled back out onto the road, grinding the gears and saying, "Sorry, sorry," as the old wreck bucked forward. Hard to tell if she was apologizing to me or to the jeep. When she got to Truman, she made a left, heading out of town.

A spring dug into my butt. I moved over to the edge of the seat and sat on one cheek. "Nice ride."

"Petra's. She's a good friend to have."

"Have you ever driven a stick shift before?"

"Once or twice. It didn't seem like the time to be buzzing around on the scooter. Someone is certain to mention seeing a pink scooter in Jon's neighborhood last night. I've tucked it away in the backyard and covered it with a tarp, just 'til this gets straightened out."

"Smart."

Lexi stopped for a light. When we stuttered our way through the intersection, she said, "Petra told me she saw you going out this morning. It was a good thing you weren't there."

"Not unexpected that the police should blame me, but I wanted Jon alive. He's the only one who knew what the hell is happening. Why did he do it, why kidnap Marley? It took nerve and planning. If it were a spur of the moment thing..." I shook my head in denial. "Who knew we were coming? I know you told Petra."

"I had to. She likes to know who she's sharing a house with. She's funny that way."

"Did you tell Dix we were coming?"

"Hell, no. Didn't even know you knew him."

"Did you tell anyone else besides Petra and Jon?"

She checked the mirrors.

"Lexi?"

"Do you think I'm responsible for this?" She spoke clearly and distinctly when she said, "I didn't tell Dix. And I don't know what's happening any more than you do."

"Did you have time last night to look at the tapes?"

"I looked at the bit from when Marley left the Rawhide with Jon until closing, all the tapes covering the outside. There was no sign of Marley or Dix." There was a silence before she added. "And Jon wasn't on the tapes either."

"Did Dix and Jon know each other?"

Her only answer was a shrug as we bucked to a stop for a red light. Lexi said, "I keep thinking…" She paused, staring straight ahead.

"What?"

"You could have been killed last night."

"Worse things than dying, Lexi."

"Like losing Marley?"

"Yeah, like losing Marley." I swiveled on the seat to look at her and the spring bit me again. "You know what I figured out?"

"What's that?"

"It's only people who are no longer afraid of dying who kill themselves — or let others do it for them. Lately, I've been thinking life wasn't worth living. Last night I found out it is. And I found out I'm still afraid of dying."

"Just remember that weird little insight the next time you get depressed."

The light had changed while we still sat there. Horns blasted behind us. Grinding gears, Lexi said, "Have you had breakfast?" and jerked through another intersection.

"No."

She made an abrupt right, accompanied by more blaring horns, and turned into a plaza. The jeep jolted to a halt in front of a little bakery with a few tables set out on the sidewalk. "Stay here, just in case there are wanted posters up for you. I'll get something." She came back with pastries and coffee and we sat in the jeep and ate while going over options. There weren't many and they weren't good.

"Why would someone kill Jon?"

"Maybe they didn't like Elvis… or maybe they did."

"Does his death make it worse for Marley or better?"

"Can't say. Can you?"

"Nope." And then I had to ask the scariest question of all. "Do you think those guys have Marley?"

Lexi dug a small white square of cardboard out of her pocket and handed it to me. "That's the number of the detective who came. Best give her a call."

"Why?"

"If you don't, she'll keep looking for you and wasting her time. Tell her about the guy you saw. She'll find him."

"You realize, of course, that will put me at the scene of the murder."

"I'm sure you can tell him about the guy that chased you without getting near the truth."

"Ah, you mean I should lie about how I know."

"If you sound like you're being up front with them, they might even believe you." She sipped at the too hot coffee. "Besides, there'll be lots of people who saw us last night."

"Did they ask you if you were there?"

"Nope."

"You mean no one has told them about the woman on the pink scooter circling the graveyard and tooting her horn?"

"Not yet." She turned to me and grinned. "It does create an image, doesn't it?"

"When they come back, tell them you were looking for a date. That will explain everything."

She swatted me with the back of her hand. "What's next?"

"If you were going to kidnap a woman in Key West, where would you hide her?" I didn't wait for her answer but plunged on with my own ideas. "It's so small and so tightly packed, there doesn't seem to be any place private enough. You couldn't hide her in a motel. Someone would see you bundling her into the room or hear her screaming or pounding her feet up

174

against a wall. And then there's the cleaning staff, so not a motel. It's a small little island with houses on top of each other. I just can't figure out where to look."

"Maybe," Lexi glanced over at me before she added, "If they keep her drugged…"

"I know." I turned my face away from her and stared out the window. "It's possible. All the more reason to come up with some place to start looking."

"Perhaps they've taken her off island."

"Miami." It was a discouraging thought. "If that's true, I haven't a chance of finding her. I'm hoping she's still here because Jon and Jodi were here."

Lex turned her cup of coffee around and around between her palms. "There's another possibility."

"And that is?"

"A boat. I listen to the VHF channel, channel sixteen. You get to hear everything that's happening on the water."

"You always loved the water. Do you have a boat?"

"Not yet, but one day. Anyway, the day you arrived there was a B.U.I. report, boating under the influence. There's a $2,500.00 fine plus community service for that."

"How does that have any connection to Marley going missing?"

"I was at the marina that afternoon. The talk was all about these two guys from Las Vegas. They had a rented boat and banged into another vessel before they were even away from the dock. They weren't drunk — just incompetent." She grimaced in disgust. "What do you expect, coming from Vegas, no water out there except maybe the Hoover Dam and that's a lot different from the Atlantic." Somewhere under the soft glow of makeup, the Florida boy who had messed around in boats his whole life, still lived. "And you found that picture of Jodi as a showgirl in Vegas."

We exchanged a glance and I said, "Maybe we're making connections that don't exist."

"Probably," Lexi said. "But have you got a better suggestion of where to start?"

"Do you know where they're anchored?"

"They rented the boat from Island's End Marina. I have a friend there. He might know."

"Let's go see if they do. I'd like to get a look at that boat."

"More breaking and entering?" She shook her head. "You never learn, do you? And just so you know, I'm doing this for Marley, not you."

"I don't care who you're doing it for, as long as it gets done."

She jerked out of the parking space and out onto the street, giving me whiplash to add to my worry list.

Land's End Marina was nearly empty of boats. Most had been put into the storage racks while others had probably been taken up the Gulf of Mexico to safer harbors.

The marina was very upscale, offering all the usual amenities, like a laundromat and supplies, but also scooter rentals and a giant pool where two men were removing the last of the chairs and tables. It was still early but the marina was busy. Boats were being hauled out of the water and onto trailers.

The warm welcome Lexi received from the manager, Vic, made it clear what had brought her to the marina on Thursday. They headed for his office, their bodies brushing up against each other.

"I know the guys you mean," he said in answer to her question. The sun had bleached his hair almost white and his skin was bronzed to the perfect tan. "I didn't have anything big enough for them."

Lewd grins and giggles before he added, "Wouldn't have rented to them anyway, but Ken Werner wasn't as picky. He needs the money. They wanted to rent his forty-two foot Hatteras Sportfish for a week. It would have brought in over three thousand dollars for the week. No worries for them, but in the end, even they realized they couldn't handle something that big and settled for his twenty-two foot. It's called the Searcher." He went to the window and looked out to see if it had been returned to its berth. "It should have been back yesterday. Ken is taking it north to get it away from the storm. It's almost too rough out there already. The storm is moving faster than predicted. His wife and her brother took the Hatteras up the Gulf yesterday. They'll be battling seas the whole way."

Lexi moved in close to him. "Do you know where the Searcher is now?"

"No, but my guess is they haven't gone far." He looked a bit worried. "Why do you want to know all of this?"

"Sherri's friend may be onboard," Lexi said, running her hand lightly across his chest. "She was supposed to be back by yesterday and hasn't called. We just want to know she's okay."

"Do you want me to try getting in touch with the Searcher?"

"Yes, please," Lexi said, her voice breathy and soft.

He tried to raise the Searcher. There was no answer. He clicked on his computer and brought up a list of names. "I'll give you Ken's number. He may know where they are, but I wouldn't call him for another couple of hours. He won't be too helpful if you wake him up. He's been busy partying."

Lexi took the slip of paper he held out. "Thanks, Vic." The smile she gifted him with was warm, very warm.

His answering grin said he felt the heat. "I'll ask around and see if anyone knows where they're anchored. I'll call you."

He didn't need to add that. I was already sure he was going to call Lexi.

"What now?" I said when we left the office and walked along the boardwalk.

"Let's wait to see if they come back in."

"We haven't got time to wait. Besides, tossing her in a tender and taking her out to a boat anchored away from a marina seems tricky for guys not used to boats. And there isn't much room to hide her on a twenty-two foot boat. The only thing that says she's with them is that they're two guys from Vegas, the same place Jodi's from."

"Give it a few hours and see what Vic comes up with, then I'll call the guy who owns the boat. In the meantime, I'm going to see if social media really works. The police would be lucky to turn out twenty people to look for Marley." She dug her phone out of her purse and set to tapping. "There are about twenty-five thousand permanent residents in Key West. With my contacts and their Facebook feeds I bet we can reach them all. That's a lot of eyes in these few square miles. I'll post the picture of Marley from the other night."

I didn't point out to her that over half the population had already left Key West. "God, I hate that a woman wearing sparkly red shorts is smarter than me."

"Always was — even before I got these great shorts." She looked up from her phone. "I asked if anyone has seen her."

"It will be Jodi they see. Tell them that she was seen around that bodega. Finding Jodi may help us find Marley because Jodi is likely the only person beside Jon who knows

179

where Marley is." I was praying Jodi knew where Marley was and was looking after her. If not, without Jon, Marley would have no food or water. Locked away and waiting for him to come back, how long could she live?

I watched a sloop called The Bristol Cutter fight its way to the mouth of the harbor, its Canadian flag snapping in the wind. Behind it a pair of dolphins arched out of the waves, sunlight gleaming on their smooth sides.

Lexi glanced up from her phone. "Call Detective McPhee while you're waiting for me."

"That isn't in the game plan."

"If you don't call, the whole damn police department will be looking for you. You won't be able to help Marley from inside a cell."

Chapter 27

Detective Ann McPhee ordered me to come in immediately.

"I was at a very late-night party. I'm still wearing the clothes I wore last night." I wanted to make it clear that I wasn't covered in blood. "Let me have a shower and I'll see you in a couple of hours." Could that buy some space without her wasting time looking for me?

"Now." Her voice said there was no wiggle room.

"All right, now." I hit End. "She wants to see me NOW."

"I'll take you," Lexi said. "But…" She looked at me over the hood of the jeep.

"What?"

"Just so you know, back in 1984 the whole Key West Police Department was declared a criminal enterprise by the Feds. Things are better these days, but they still aren't cops you want to smart mouth." She put away her phone and got into the driver's seat, but didn't start the engine. "For once in your life will you please be…" Lexi lifted her shoulders and let them fall. "Well, just don't be your normal in-your-face smart ass."

"Thank you for your advice, Lexi. I'll endeavor to live up to your standards."

She pounded her fist on the steering wheel. "See, there you go already. Be as polite as you would to your granny. Dab at your eyes and play at demure. You do know what that word means, don't you?"

"Dim you are, yup, got it."

The police department has its headquarters on Roosevelt Boulevard in a pink building with a two-story rotunda on the front. Really, how seriously can you take cops whose offices are in a pink building and whose motto is Protecting Paradise? Surely, I'd be able to finesse a small-town cop. The notice on the door said KWPD was part of a High Intensity Drug Trafficking Area (HIDTA). Okay, maybe they were a little more serious than the building. While we waited for McPhee I read a little sign with the history of the KWPD. Originally, Key West had a marshal and the jail was the brig of a ship. What kept the prisoners from jumping overboard and swimming ashore? I mean besides sharks and killer currents.

"Ms. Travis?"

I turned to face Detective Ann McPhee. The little voice in my head said, *Oh, oh, Sugar, this ain't gonna be easy.* "No nonsense" were the first words that came to mind — and nonsense and horseshit was all I had to give her. Wearing a severe black pant suit with a pale mauve blouse, her one concession to her gender, she was about five feet seven and muscular with clever blue eyes had spent thousands of hours watching for weaknesses and lies. Following her down a corridor, I could already feel handcuffs closing around my wrists.

In a small Spartan room, a space designed to make guests feel unwelcome and uncomfortable, and with air conditioning blowing like a February cold spell, she pointed to a hard-wooden chair and said, "Sit."

When I'd done as she commanded, she sat down behind the bare desk and contemplated me. "All right, now tell me what you know about Jon Kidd."

"I met him Thursday night at the Rawhide." I told her most of the story. I ended with, "I didn't kill him."

"Jon Kidd called the station and said you threatened him."

"Really?"

"Plus, you told one of our officers that you weren't going to let him leave Key West." She frowned at me. "How were you planning on stopping him?"

I sat there trying to think of an answer. I had none. "I didn't kill him. How could he tell me where Marley was if I killed him?"

"Tell me again about going to his house."

"I was there in the morning and went back later that day and hung about, looking for Marley."

"Playing detective." She didn't try to hide her disgust.

183

"Marley was missing and the cops weren't doing anything. Are you treating her as a missing person now?"

"She's a person of interest in Jon Kidd's death."

"What?"

"You say she was with him and now she's missing. I want to hear what she knows about him."

"She hasn't been anywhere near his house since she left to have dinner with him."

"What makes you so sure?"

"I didn't see her there." A lame answer that didn't impress McPhee. "I didn't see her go in or leave."

"Did you see anyone there?"

"I saw two guys come to the house." It was a lie but not much of one. "It was about ten. Soon after they arrived, I heard the shower start up."

"Would you know them if you saw them again?"

"I'm not sure. It was dark. They were both big and they were driving a beige sedan."

She frowned at me. "That's not much."

"Oh, pardon me. I didn't know you wanted me to play detective. I would have paid closer attention and taken notes."

McPhee glared at me. I slid my spine down into the hard chair.

"A motorist reported a big man chasing a woman into the cemetery last night. He almost hit the woman so he was able to give us an excellent description of her."

184

"That's good." I nodded, trying to convince her of my sincerity.

McPhee reached below her desk top and opened a drawer. She brought out a baggie and set it carefully in the middle of the desk. "Do you know what this key is for?" She slid it toward me, lifted her fingers off the baggie, and sat back, waiting.

I stared at the key in the small evidence bag. "Where'd it come from?"

She frowned. "Do you know what it opens?"

I leaned forward. "Is it for a bicycle lock? I didn't see a bike in Jon's backyard but if he didn't own a bike or a scooter he's the only one in Key West who doesn't. Maybe it's for a shed, but there wasn't one of those in his back yard either." If it was in Jon's pocket was it for the place he'd hidden Marley? "Was it Jon's key?"

"So, you have no idea what this key is for?"

"It looks like the one for the padlock on my gym locker. Did Jon have a locker somewhere? Did he have a locker at work?"

There was a knock on the door. I turned to see a man in a rumpled suit motioning to McPhee. The grim look on his face had McPhee getting quickly to her feet. She left the room without comment, temporarily forgetting about me.

My gut clenched. Something had happened, something involving Jon's death and therefore Marley. I'd know soon enough what it was. I turned back to the key, positive that they'd found it on Jon and just as convinced that it would open the lock to Marley's prison. When hope is running out you'll cling to anything. Time was also in short supply. If he'd locked her away without food or water, how many days could she last? I needed that key.

Not for a moment did I worry that I was making the hunt for Jon's killer more difficult. My only concern was finding Marley and being able to free her from wherever she was being held.

If I got caught stealing evidence, they'd arrest me. That would be tricky. It would take hours, maybe even a whole day to get bailed out. My brain argued both sides, trying to make up my mind. I watched in fascination as my hand stole toward the baggie, saw my fingers pick it up, felt the slick cool plastic and then the hard outline of the key as my hand closed around it. All the while, my brain was still saying, *Don't do it, don't do it.*

Still, it was no crime to just pick it up. I could still put it down and walk away. My hand clutched it tightly, drawing it toward me. And then it deposited the key deep in my pocket before it settled back in my lap, waiting. The desktop looked horribly empty. As soon as she came back McPhee was going to see the bag was gone. I was up that proverbial creek. Should I leave before she returned? She would come after me. I reached in my pocket and brought out the small sheet of ragged paper on which I'd written the phone number that was left on the Sunset's answering service. The desk didn't look empty anymore. The yellow note stood out like a beacon. My hands went to the armrest and I gathered myself to rise to my feet.

The door opened behind me. I settled back down, prepared for the worst. But McPhee didn't go behind the desk. She sat on the corner of it and looked intently down at me, so close I could smell her scent, an expensive perfume. "Do you know your friend's blood type?"

Bile flowed up my throat. I swallowed. "Why?"

"Answer my question." Her words were abrupt but her voice was softer, filled with concern that hadn't been there at the beginning of our interview. "Do you know Marley's blood type?"

"Not until you tell me why." In the final year of high school a bloodmobile had parked behind Jacaranda High and all the seniors went out to donate. We were so young we didn't realize how few blood types there were in the world, so Marley and I had thought it was an important mark of our friendship when we discovered we had the same one.

The line of McPhee's mouth thinned. This was a woman who was accustomed to being in charge. She didn't take well to my feeble attempt to push back. Her lips pursed, working on spitting out an order. Finally, she gave in. "Blood was found in the back of Jon's SUV."

I could only shake my head in denial. McPhee's voice was almost gentle when she asked, "What blood type was she?"

187

"Was? Have you found a body?" A lump of dread landed in my stomach. I could hardly croak out the words, "Like me, she was A Positive."

McPhee's poker face didn't hold. Her indifference was gone.

"No," I said, and rose, holding out a hand to stave off what she might say. "It isn't Marley's." More than ever, I needed to get away from here, away from what McPhee was suggesting. "You're wrong."

"I didn't say it was her blood. That's why we need a sample of her DNA." The hard lines of her face softened as she rose from the desk and stepped toward me, her hand held out for comfort or support, but I backed away.

"Marley isn't dead." I stumbled farther back from her.

"We need a sample of Marley's DNA, a toothbrush or a hairbrush will do."

"You're not listening. Marley isn't dead. I'd know if she was." I pivoted toward the door.

"Where are you going?" she barked.

"Back to Lexi's."

"No, you're not." Her compassion hadn't lasted long. She was back in her in-charge mode and ready to make me fall in line. "Come back and sit down."

I looked over my shoulder at her but I didn't stop sliding away. "Am I under arrest?"

"No." It was a painful admission.

"Then I'm leaving." I reached for the doorknob.

"Don't leave Key West."

"I'm not going anywhere without Marley." I couldn't make the door work, pushing instead of pulling, before crashing into the frame on the way out. Frantic, and on the edge of a meltdown, I shot into the hall, nearly running in my haste to get away. Halfway down the hall I heard a man behind me, calling my name. I hesitated, then hurried on without looking back until I felt the hand on my arm, holding me there. I slapped at it, screaming, "Don't touch me." Telling this giant cop not to touch me was laughable. If the uniformed officer was going to arrest me for stealing a key, his hand on my arm would be the least of it.

He said, "I'll escort you out of the building."

"What?" Over his shoulder, I saw McPhee watching us. "Why?" I'd tell them I hadn't stolen the key, had only picked it up to look closer at it, but when McPhee told me about the blood I was so shocked that I'd forgotten I was holding the key and had taken it by mistake. With a lie ready, I calmed down a little. "You don't have to show me out of this shit hole. I know the way."

"Visitors aren't allowed to roam the building unescorted."

"Okay, okay, but hurry." I jogged away from him.

We were nearly to the exit when he asked, "May I have your pass, please?" Barely hesitating in my charge toward

189

freedom, I pulled it from around my neck and tossed it toward him.

I burst through the front door and trotted across the parking lot, forgetting all about Lexi, and just wanting to distance myself from that pink building. A hundred yards away from the station, a horn blasted beside me.

I kept walking. If they wanted me they needed to do more than use their horn. I was done with them. They weren't going to help me. I had to do this on my own. And cold sober.

The jeep pulled in beside me. "Hey, Crazy Woman, wait."

I bent over at the knees, taking deep breaths. "Hop in," Lexi said.

When I was in I said, "Just drive." And then I added, "Fast."

The jeep stuttered forward. "What did you do?" There were no flies on Lexi. She'd already figured out the cops were coming for me.

I huddled down against the door. There were so many things I should have told the police. I should go back. If I hadn't stolen the key, if they hadn't talked about finding Marley's blood...

I hadn't thought it through.

Chapter 28

The wind had picked up. There was evidence everywhere of the coming storm. Simple things, from flowers and leaves ripped from their bushes to stop signs fluttering—it all said, "Get ready. I'm about to kick the shit out of you." Down on the beach the waves would be a good six feet higher than normal, every surfer's dream. Duval Street would be rocking with thrill seekers catching a big one and excited newcomers in town to experience the storm. There's a fool for every occasion. People always underestimate how bad it can be and instead of being frightened, they're thrilled by the idea of being in a storm like Alma.

Lexi said, "Let's go home. I need to hear everything."

I didn't lift my head when I said, with defeat in my voice, "No, the police will be there soon looking for me."

"I thought they just released you."

"It won't last."

"Why?" I could hear the laughter in her voice. "Are you escaping custody?"

"No, they weren't holding me." I pivoted on the seat to watch her as I added, "I stole a key."

"What?" The jeep veered into oncoming traffic. Horns blared. When she was back in the correct lane, Lexi screamed, "Why?"

I couldn't answer because I was still braced against the door, still holding my breath and waiting for the impact of a head-on collision. "Why?" she asked again.

My panic had veered from one terrifying catastrophe to another. I pointed down the street and said, "Watch the road," and then took a very deep breath while my heart settled to a more normal rhythm.

"Why would you steal something from a police station? God damn it, Sherri…"

"I think Jon had it on him when they found his body. I figure it's the key to the place he hid Marley."

"Jesus," she said. She was still upset, but at least this time she didn't try to kill anyone. "You're in serious trouble!"

As if I didn't know. "I'll tell them I picked it up to see if I could identify it and I forgot it was in my hand."

"Good, very good." She nodded her head. "Got your lies already lined up. That's good. You're a pro at this shit. But what if they find Marley and you have the key?"

"They'll use bolt cutters. I don't have bolt cutters."

I let her calm down a bit more before I said, "There's more."

Cars honked behind us as the jeep shuddered to a near halt and then careened around a corner, slamming to a stop in the middle of a side street. "More? What more? Is it Marley?" Lexi demanded. "What the hell is happening?"

"They found blood in Jon's vehicle."

She inhaled sharply. I watched her face as she bit down on her lip. "Just because they found blood, that doesn't mean it's Marley's." That was the thing about Lexi, knock her down and she bounced right back up.

"That's what I said." I looked away from the alarm on her face, and stared out the window at a pretty house covered in bougainvillea. "I'm sure it was her blood type. I think there must be a fast way of checking for blood type because when I told them Marley was A positive they immediately wanted a DNA sample."

"Oh." We sat there in silence until Lexi sighed and said, "So what do you want to do?" Her phone rang. She looked at the number and said, "Hi, Vic." She listened a minute and then said, "I know where it is." She glanced over at me. "I can't. Have a safe trip." She hit End. "Those two guys are back at the marina, sunburned and bitching about not catching any fish. They're taking the last flight out of Key West, flying out in an hour. Do you want to go talk to them?"

"The only thing to tie them to Marley is that they arrived from Las Vegas the day before she disappeared. There's nothing more than that to connect them to Jodi or Jon."

"Yes..." She thought it over and then sighed in a defeated sort of way. "When you asked me where I'd hide someone, I thought of a boat." She sighed. "Vic said they were alone when they got off the boat and he checked it out when they left the marina. There was no sign of Marley."

193

"I think Jon was the one who hid Marley. Not those guys or anyone else." I reached down and touched the key in my pocket. "It was an idea."

She drummed her blood-red nails on the steering wheel. "Have you figured out why Marl was kidnapped?"

"I think so. That Las Vegas picture... I'm betting he wanted Marley to stand in for Jodi. Does that make sense?"

"As far as it goes. But why?"

"Interesting question, but I doubt knowing the answer will help us figure out where he hid her. He didn't have much time to organize it. He only saw her that night and the next day she was gone."

"I showed him that picture of you and Marley on Tuesday. I saw the change in him, saw his excitement when he saw the picture, but I thought it was because he fancied his chances." She wiped her hands down her face.

I turned away and watched a man fasten a piece of plywood over his front window. He probably kept them under his porch to pull out and fasten in place whenever gale force winds threatened. When the drill whined that the screw was in as far as it was going he climbed slowly down from the ladder. Would he stay inside his boarded-up home or was he going to leave when the last piece of plywood was in place? Many people who try to ride out a hurricane drown in their own homes.

We sat there in silence for some time. Finally, Lexi started the engine, ground it into reverse, and jerked backwards.

A horn blared. Crosswise in the traffic, blocking both lanes, she fought with the transmission.

"Do you want me to drive?" I asked.

"No, God damn it." The jeep coughed its way forward and died with two wheels up on the sidewalk. "I'm sorry," she said and laid her head down on the steering wheel. Her shoulders were shaking with sobs.

She raised her head, sniffed and wiped her nose. Mascara ran down her cheeks in black rivulets. "What do we do now?"

"It's what happened before he went to Il Paradiso that we need to know about. I'm sure that the person the waiter described wasn't Marley. Jon had already hidden her by then."

Lexi leaned forward and studied the sky through the windshield. "I hope he told someone where she is. They've changed the forecast from tropical storm to possible hurricane winds. That means winds of a hundred miles an hour and more rain." She swung to face me. Her makeup was wrecked now, something out of a horror movie. "The weather channel has been going on about the fact there's a full moon. That will deliver super high tides... hurricane winds and rain..."

She didn't have to finish. Lexi was thinking the same thing I was. Even with only a tropical storm we would have had a lot of flooding. If Marley was outside, locked in a shed or under a house or even on the ground floor of a house, she could drown.

195

I could smell rain. The air was heavy with it. And the wind... Not long now.

Chapter 29

14 hours before Alma hits

My phone rang. When I said, "Hello," Tanya started in without preamble. "Marley's credit card was used at a bodega in Key West today. Seems your friend is avoiding you."

"That's nonsense. Someone has her card. Likely Jodi."

"That's all I can tell you." She didn't even say goodbye.

I stared at the silent phone as if Tanya might still be there and could help me make sense out of the improbable. For one second I wondered if it was true, if Marley was actually out there walking around while I went crazy. Was she trying to teach me some stupid lesson?

I didn't believe it for a minute. If Marley had a problem with me or with Lexi, this wasn't how she'd handle it. She's the loud and vocal type. Besides, her clothes and her car were here. She'd at least want them even if she'd had enough of us.

"Let's go to Rude George's. I want to talk to everyone who ever met Jon. Somewhere there's a padlock that fits this key. When we find that, we'll find Marley."

The gears of the jeep ground and the heap of rust shot forward and died up against a purple shrub. There was the distinct smell of something burning. One more thing to worry about.

Lexi reached down to retrieve her sandals from the floor, and opened her door. Still barefoot, she came around to my side and said, "Get over."

The jeep behaved like a dream. At the next cross-street we waited for a line of cars that were loaded up to, and on top of, the roof. Everything that was portable and important was packed into the car with the family. The evacuation route out of the Keys would be full and all the roads leading to Key West would be closed by now, allowing for northbound traffic only.

A sedan with a black lab panting out the window hesitated in front of us. The lab barked excitedly. The woman in the passenger seat beside the dog hauled it back in by the collar and raised the window. We pulled in behind them and made the slow crawl to the next cross street. Traffic was backed up all the way to the beach. Crossing was impossible. It gave Lexi lots of time to repair the damage that the tears had done.

A horn honked behind us. I took my foot off the brake, crept forward five feet, and stopped again. A woman carrying a small crying child stepped off the sidewalk in front of me. She brushed her windblown hair out of her face and gave a small wave of her hand before she zigged through the traffic to the sidewalk on the opposite side of the road.

I stared at the red taillights in front of me and said, "Look, Lex, if you want to evacuate with the rest of Key West, go ahead."

"Is that what you think of me?" Her voice was soft and terribly sad.

I risked a glance in her direction. She looked calm and resigned as she said, "You think I'm going to run out and leave you here on your own?"

I made a left in front of a driver who was more worried about his paint job than I was about the jeep.

Lexi said, "I don't give a shit what you think of me. I'm not going anywhere." She shook her forefinger under my nose. "And just you remember, she's my friend too and I'm just as scared as you are. Well, you aren't the important one here. It's about Marley, not you."

Normally Rude George's was open to the street on two sides, just one giant tiki hut. Now heavy steel barriers had been rolled down to keep out the wind. When we'd passed it yesterday, it had been jumping. Now the crowd was sparse, but the people who were still here were making the most of their time before evacuating, even as workers loaded tables and chairs onto a truck parked on the street. The furniture would head up towards Miami for safety with all the last-minute evacuees.

Overhead, the ceiling was still covered in palm fronds and fairy lights, and the giant fans were still turning. Wooden parrots in bright colors still swung on perches high under the peaked roof, and Reggae music filled the air. When we were halfway across the room, Lexi caught the eye of a waiter and pointed questioningly to the back. He nodded in reply. At the end of the bar, shoved into a corner where the door to the kitchen opened and closed, was a small table. It was the worst table in the house if you came to enjoy the entertainment, but the very best if you came to solicit information from the staff. Sooner or later everyone who worked there would go by. The waiter Lexi had nodded to followed us with a tray full of empty glasses. He slid the tray onto the bar and came over. "What do you need, Lex?"

She twisted around on her chair and asked, "Do you want a drink, Sherri?"

"God, yes!" I quickly followed that with, "No, if I have a drink…" I took a deep breath and let it out slowly. If I had a drink that would be the end of looking for Marley. *No need to share that nasty truth.* I hid my shaking hands beneath the Mexican tiled tabletop. "A coffee please."

When the waiter left, Lexi said, "One drink won't hurt, might do you good."

"Ha! You know me, Lexi. One is just the beginning of a long night. We'll have a drink when Marley gets back."

"Okay," She looked around and pointed. "There's Gary. He's the manager. We'll start with him." Even barefoot, Lexi stands nearly six feet tall, and today she was wearing high heeled sandals so she towered over everyone else in the place. Even without the height she would be hard to miss. Wearing those red sparkly short shorts, with an equally tiny tank top, she threaded her way through the packed tables toward a harried looking man working a table of tourists who seemed to be complaining. Heads turned as she passed. When she got to Gary it took a bit of convincing to get him to come talk to us. Finally, Lexi strutted back to me, easing her way through the tables, and giving me a thumbs-up.

Gary didn't look cool enough to work at Rude George's. In Key West, when you go in and out of the restaurants and bars, it seems all the serving staff were hired because they look good. Not this guy. He wore gold rimmed glasses that were years out of date, had thinning hair beyond severe widow's peaks, and was way overweight from a life of continuously available fries.

Gary wasn't happy to see us, but then nothing had made him happy for a long time. He pulled out a chair and collapsed onto it. He was probably only in his mid-thirties, but he already seemed well past middle age. The tropical floral shirt, worn outside his black slacks, was less successful than he might be hoping for in his attempt to hide his paunch while trying to look hip. "I'm sorry your friend is missing." His fingers massaged his left temple. "Quiet little thing."

"I've never heard anyone describe Marley as quiet," I said.

He lifted his shoulders and then let them slump back down. "I only met her for a minute when she came in with Jon, but I'm happy to help all I can."

"Thanks, Gary," Lexi said. "Who did Jon socialize with outside of work?"

"No one special." Gary didn't seem very upset by Jon's death. Watching him, I decided all Gary was feeling was tired. "It was his first time working here and it was only a six-week gig. Not a lot of time to make friends." He grimaced. "A performer's life is hell, moving all the time, always on the road."

I leaned forward. "But he had worked in Key West before, hadn't he?"

"Yeah, every year, at different places. Sometimes he was here more than once a year. The tourists loved him. He had a good reputation for drawing the crowds and being dependable. But the night before he died, he came in late for his last show and only did half of it."

I was fixated on finding connections. "So, he probably knew people here."

He thought about it for a minute and nodded. "That's true. Lots of people who'd seen him before came to the shows and a few people came just to hang out with him. I guess he picked up where he left off last time he was here."

"Was he friendly with anyone working here?"

"Everyone. He was that kind of guy, chatty and happy to see you. Well-liked and always included in after-hours things. He was here off and on from opening until closing so he didn't have too much time for anyone not working here."

"It's the same everywhere. My wait-staff hang out together after work and play golf together in the morning before work, nine holes on Mondays and Wednesdays."

The waiter brought our coffee and as he set it down Gary said, "Simon, didn't you go diving with Jon?"

"Yeah…" Uncertain and cautious, Simon looked from Lexi to me, wondering where this was going, his body language saying he didn't want to get tangled up in anyone else's bad news.

Gary stood up. "Lexi and her friend want to speak to you about Jon."

Simon scowled. "It was just one of those tourist things, an hour in a pool with scuba tanks and then a few hours fooling around a wreck."

Holding onto the back of his chair, Gary pointed to it and said, "Sit down for a minute and talk to them. I'll pick up your tables."

Simon sank into the chair, brushing back a fall of fine blond hair. Tall and thin, Simon could almost pass for a teenager, but his were the kind of fine Nordic looks that would go fast when they started to slip. He said, "I can't believe anyone would murder Jon. Dude, seriously? This is Key West. That sort of thing doesn't happen here."

The coffee I'd just sipped turned to acid in my stomach. There it was again, someone thinking they had a special dispensation from crime. Lexi clutched my arm, her red nails digging in. She leaned forward, putting her body between mine and his. "I know, Simon, it's a shock. We're all shattered. But Sherri's friend is missing and no one can find her. We think Jon knew what happened to her."

Lexi let go of my hand but she didn't move aside. I picked up the coffee. My shaking hands sent the brew spilling over the brim. I set it down again. Lexi said, "We need your help. You probably knew Jon better than anyone here."

He bit down on his lip and looked away. "Please," Lexi said.

"I don't know anything that could help you. Ask Gary, he's the boss." I watched Simon's face, saw the sly pleasure his secrets were giving him.

Lexi gave a soft trill of laughter and settled back in her chair. "Oh, go away. Gary knows nothing but the work schedule. The guys in charge never do, but I bet you can pretty much guess at what Jon got up to." She wiggled her shoulders and gave him a smile that would make him give up his granny. "You and I know how things work."

He worried his lip and then the left corner of his mouth twitched and a smile slid across his face. "He didn't just entertain the tourists in here." He leaned closer and looked around, making sure he wasn't being overheard. "He entertained them elsewhere. The ladies liked him and he wasn't adverse to spending an hour or two pleasing them."

"I'm sure they rewarded him handsomely."

"They bought him stuff. Sometimes they even gave him money." His eyes searched the room for his boss. Easy to see Jon wasn't the only one who helped the ladies out, which probably explained why they'd become friends. Together, one blond and one dark, out on the prowl they must have made quite a pair.

I joined the conversation. "Was there anyone special he was seeing?"

"Mostly just tourists."

"He must have known some people from when he stayed here before."

Simon nodded. "He had one special friend here in Key West. He saw her a couple of times a week."

"What's her name?"

Lexi's phone rang. She looked at the call display and smiled. "This might be it." She stood up, turning away from the table. Simon and I waited and listened to monosyllabic responses until Lexi swung around and gave me a thumbs-up. "Tell me that address again." She made scrambling motions with her hand and Simon handed over his pen while I smoothed out a napkin for her to write on. "We've got her," Lexi said as she hit End.

Chapter 30

Lexi dumped the phone in her purse and pulled out a few bills. "Thanks, Simon." She yanked her purse up onto her arm and pushed past him, but I had one more question. "Did you ever meet Jon's sister?"

"I knew he had one, but no, I never met her." Simon stood up, eager to be away.

I got to my feet reluctantly and pushed the chair in, feeling I hadn't asked the right questions. "Did you know she was in Key West?"

His eyebrows rose. "Do you think she killed Jon?" It was a good question and one I'd never considered. I asked, "Did he tell you where she was staying?"

He was already walking away but he replied, "Didn't even tell me she was here." He seemed put out enough that it might even be true.

"Thanks," I said and scooted around an empty table, hurrying to catch up with Lexi.

"Tell me," I said, as I got behind the wheel and pulled the door shut.

"Jodi's right where you said she would be. Near the bodega." I started the engine and edged the jeep out into traffic as Lexi continued, "One of the Bitch & Stitch group lives in an efficiency motel and says Jodi moved in there last week. Keagan has only seen her twice, and that was at night, but he says it's her for sure. He says she doesn't want to be seen. When he tried to talk to her, she scurried into her unit and closed the door. It's her."

"Great."

"We have to tell the cops."

"And we will. Right after we talk to her."

Lexi jerked her head around to give me a look. "Truth?"

"Sure."

With Lexi giving directions, we fought our way through Key West traffic. The town was on the move.

The motel was at the end of a shaded alley called Poor Man's Lane, an oyster-shell track sliced off the back lawn of an old estate. An enchanting place of leaning fences, houses in bleached pastels and a trumpet vine overtaking an oak tree, its few dwellings had fallen into cheerful decay. When we got out of the jeep, it felt almost cool under the leafy canopy that danced above us in the strengthening winds.

At the dead-end crouched a little L-shaped Munchkin motel. The center of the lane had been taken over by several lounge chairs and a patio set. Huge baskets of staghorn ferns swayed from the overhanging trees as a cheerful beach towel blew toward us. Lexi reached down and picked it up and dropped it on a lounger with other stray pieces of clothing. The place had a feel of companionable sociability, a casual intimacy shaped by people passing through, easy friendships picked up and then set aside just as quickly in a community that flowed and altered. There were only nine units, easy to see how you'd know your neighbor, and yet it was still a great place to hide out, private and with a great garden to sit in to keep you from going crazy.

The aluminum screen door squeaked open and Keagan stepped out before we could knock. Bare chested and bare footed, I recognized him from the dark soul patch under his bottom lip, one of the dancing waiters from the Rawhide. "Hi," he said, grinning at me like we knew each other real well — and maybe we did. My memory of that night had great big holes in it but I was sure that he'd seen enough of me to justify his smirk.

"Hi." I tried to smile. "Where is she?"

He pointed. "The last unit."

"Thanks."

Lexi and Keagan followed me as I walked down the line of rentals. I stopped and turned to them. "You don't have to come."

"Try and stop me," Lexi said, but then she turned to Keagan and said. "Thanks, Hon. Why don't you wait inside for us?"

"You might need some muscle," Keagan replied.

They discussed it while I went to the door of number five and tried the door handle. Locked. I started pounding.

"Jodi, open up. I'm a friend of Jon's. He told me where you were."

No answer.

"You need help. I'm here to help you." I moved to the window but the curtains were pulled tightly together with no opening to peer through. "Let's talk, Jodi. The storm is coming. You need to get out of here."

The door opened a crack and two eyes peered out. We stared at each other. It was like looking at Marley, or more correctly, a ghost of the person I knew so well. I pushed on the door and the opening widened a little, but she wasn't ready to let me in.

"I don't know you." Wary and frightened she tried to close the door.

I put my shoulder through the opening. "Do you know anyone in Key West?" She didn't answer. "So, let me in. You're in trouble. You've got to trust someone."

She sighed and opened the door all the way. I stepped inside. The one room efficiency, filled with cheap furniture, was saved from drabness by tropical prints in every color of the spectrum. The room was air-conditioned into the sixties and, after the outside temperature that was nearly ninety, I shivered from the shock of it. But maybe it wasn't just the temperature. She was a couple of inches taller than Marley, wearing a white denim skirt, frayed at the bottom, a white tee with cherries all over it and Roman sandals in soft black suede. Her hair was darker and straight and was caught up in a scrunchy. Marley and Jodi looked enough alike to be twins. And yet, there was a subtle difference. I watched her turn away and walk ten paces to the far edge of the room and then turn back to study me.

They were twins in the pictures, but different in reality. Why? Bearing and attitude mostly, Jodi carried herself like a Vegas showgirl. Her walk and poise were totally at odds with the way Marley zipped around, always in a hurry, her movements fast and jerky. Darting from one place to another, I'm sure she never gave a thought to how others saw her. Not this woman. She was totally tuned into the impression she delivered, monitoring it and assessing the onlooker's reaction. Even in this situation, there was a sense of surety about Jodi, a confidence that she could handle whatever came and that she was perfect just the way she was. Did she know her brother had been murdered? If so, she was well in control of her emotions, and the calculating expression on her face was saying she was figuring out an angle, deciding how she could spin this and use me. Marley would never have the cold selfishness I was looking at.

McPhee had said a woman reported Jon's murder. "You know about Jon." I wasn't sure if I was asking a question or stating a reality. "You called the police."

"What's it to you?"

That was it. I went off like a rocket. Anxiety and horror were like an acid eating through my self-control. I shot toward her, slapping her across the face and then pushing her down onto an easy chair.

Indignant and angry, she tried to get up. "What the hell..." It was all she got out before I hit her again. I leaned in close and hissed, "Listen to me, you bitch, your brother kidnapped my friend." The smell of expensive perfume rose from her. "I want to know where she is and if you don't tell me you're..." I had no idea what I'd do. I just knew that any restraint I'd ever possessed was well and truly lost and I was now capable of anything.

Her defiant chin jutted out. "I have no idea what you're talking about."

"Don't you? That's a shame, because after I beat the shit out of you I'm going to turn you over to Detective McPhee. I'm sure she'll have some questions about your brother's murder."

"I didn't do it."

"Tell it to McPhee. And there's another thing. Whatever scheme Jon was involved in, you were in it up to your neck and perhaps, just perhaps, whoever killed Jon may be looking for you. I intend to lead them right to you, give them you in exchange for Marley."

I had her attention now. The confidence went out of her face. Fear replaced it. "You wouldn't do that." There was something, or someone, she dreaded more than the police and more than me.

"Try me. I'll do anything it takes."

She stiffened, knowing my words were true.

"Where is she?" I demanded.

"I don't know where she is. I don't know why Jon took her."

"Don't give me that shit. He was substituting Marley for you. Where is she?"

She shook her head. "He said the less I knew the better it would be for me. He just gave me her clothes and her purse and told me to come to Rude George's. He didn't want me to talk too much to anyone. Then we went to the restaurant. After that, I was to come back here and stay out of sight until he came for me. He was supposed to be here by midnight. We were going up to Miami and then we were going to disappear."

"Why do you need to disappear?"

She crossed her arms and made a face. I grabbed her by the hair and slammed her head back. "Why?"

Her hands shot up to cover mine. Pain filled her face but I didn't let go. I shook her head violently while her nails dug into my hand. Strangely, while I knew her fingers were clawing at me, I couldn't feel anything. I just went on screaming, "Where is she?" and shaking her. My left hand went to her throat. She moaned, "Stop, stop, I'll tell you. But let go of me."

I took my hands away but I didn't step back. She started with the sniffles and tears but she wasn't speaking.

"Look," I said. "I saw those two big brutes that killed Jon. They aren't going to back off. Shall I call them and tell them where to find you?"

She glared at me and rubbed her head. "I was working as a show girl in Vegas and living with this guy, a gambler and a drug dealer."

I hadn't even noticed that Lexi had come into the room behind me until she said, "Smart move."

"Shut up, Lexi." I didn't take my eyes off Jodi. "I only want to know about Marley." I grabbed Jodi by her hair again. "What does this have to do with kidnapping Marley?"

"I stole some coke," she screamed. Her hands covered mine, trying to pull them away. "It's worth a lot of money, over three million dollars."

"And?"

Her fingers pulled at mine. "You're hurting me."

"Yes, and I'll hurt you a lot more. What happened?"

"Jon was here in Key West so that's where I came to hide. Giovanni doesn't know anything about Jon, at least I don't remember telling him about Jon, so I don't know how they found him. Maybe he was killed for some other reason."

"Not likely. Keep talking. I want to know everything."

She rubbed her head where I'd held her hair. "Giovanni thought I was stupid and too afraid of him to ever try to put one over on him. It made him careless." A sly smile. "I planned it well, ran with nothing. Left everything behind except what I had

213

in my purse. I only used cash so they couldn't track my credit cards and even destroyed my phone in case they could track that." She went over what she'd believed to be the perfect plan. "I stole the van, loaded with two hundred kilos of cocaine, that Giovanni had hidden in a storage unit. I had at least six hours before they would even know I was gone. I drove right through, sleeping in the van, and called Jon from Tampa. We met in Miami. Jon transferred the drugs to his car and took the plate off the van, and ditched it."

"Did Jon know what you were planning?"

"Nope. Not until I called him from Tampa. I didn't want him to know in case they got to him before I did." She tilted her head and frowned. "He was really, really, angry. But he wanted some of the money and he should have been safe. Giovanni didn't know about him. I just can't figure out how they found him."

"Who did you list as your next of kin on your employee record?"

Her eyes got big and she said, "Oh."

"All they had to do was call and say you'd been in an accident and needed to know your next of kin. They have his information."

"Shit." She beat her fists against her knees in fury at her own stupidity.

"So then what?"

"They found Jon almost as soon as I arrived. A guy grabbed Jon off the street when I was out buying clothes. He put a gun to Jon's head and wanted to know where to find me. Jon said he didn't know where I was if I wasn't in Vegas. This guy told him that he had to turn me over or they'd kill him. They gave him a deadline to find me."

I stepped back. "And then what?"

"I couldn't go back to Jon's so I came here. Jon stayed here last year."

"When did he decide to take Marley?"

"When he saw the picture of your friend he decided to substitute her for me to give us time to get away. He made me promise to share the money from the sale of the drugs with him, fifty-fifty. But it was me that took all the risks and set everything up." She seemed really annoyed by her brother cutting into her revenue. "He went to the Rawhide and saw Marley. She looked enough like me to pass so we went ahead with the plan."

"Where is she now? What did he do with her?"

"I don't know."

If she was telling the truth, finding Jodi had put me no closer to finding Marley. "What about the drugs? Where are they?"

She started to cry. "I don't know."

Chapter 31

I believed Jodi when she said she didn't know where the drugs were. She was too devastated at their loss to be lying, but I wasn't sure she didn't know where Marley was. "What about these guys looking for you, how well do they know you? Is Giovanni one of them?"

"No. He probably hired two goons from Miami." That sly smile slipped across her face again. "He's in deep trouble, trying to convince his partners he isn't part of this. No way he'd dare leave Vegas. I was counting on that. If he saw your friend he'd know in a minute she wasn't me. It wouldn't work if Giovanni showed up."

She drew her knees up to her chest. "Jon said those guys had a picture of me, so I likely don't know them. Anyway, Jon said my resemblance to your friend was close enough that they wouldn't be able to tell the difference." It was true. Even I could have been fooled if I'd only had a quick glimpse. From a picture, even if they'd met Jodi a few times, they wouldn't have been able to tell the difference between the two women. "The color of the hair was wrong. He was going to tell them I'd dyed my hair when he delivered the girl." She said it like he would be handing over a bundle of dirty laundry.

I leaned toward her, wanting to see her face, needing to know the worst they had planned. "And then what? What was supposed to happen after that?"

She rubbed her head and then drew her fingers through her hair, smoothing it and styling it. "I didn't stay with Jon, Jon was smart, wouldn't let me." Just that quickly, her self-possession had returned and she was no longer concerned about me. "He found me this place, got me some food and told me to stay here until he came for me."

"Don't change the subject. What was Jon planning? How was he going to make the substitution?"

"I don't know." Her voice had gone high and whiny, wanting to excuse herself. "I'm not even sure he did. I just knew he was going to pass her off as me while we split."

"Would he kill her? Turn over a dead body?"

Her eyes couldn't meet mine. "God, no. Jon would never hurt anyone." She was saying it but I wasn't really believing the words. Neither was she. We both knew that when people get desperate, things go wrong. "Why would you think such a thing?" she asked, all innocent shock. The last time this woman had been innocent she'd still been drinking from a sippy cup.

"You see, I have a problem with what you're telling me," I said. "I don't see how Jon could hope to get away with it if Marley was alive. The substitution would have worked until Marley opened her mouth. She'd yell like a banshee. If they skyped your boyfriend he'd know it wasn't you right away, your voices are completely different. And of course, Marley wouldn't know what they were talking about. At most, it would have worked for a day — if Marley were alive. Still, you look enough alike, if they'd sent a picture of a dead woman to your boyfriend, he would have confirmed that it was you."

She drew her legs up under her. Huddling down in the chair, she started rocking back and forth.

"Your boyfriend wouldn't let you walk away from this alive, would he?"

She rocked harder.

"Not even if you gave back the drugs?"

She shook her head. "He'd kill me. That's what Jon said."

"So, he needed a body to substitute for you."

"Jon told me I was stupid to steal the drugs, but he was trying to help me. If it was your friend's life or mine, what would you expect him to do?"

Somehow in her mind that justified murder, her life being more important than Marley's. "Did you sample the goods?"

Her only response was to curl up tighter.

"Sure, you did." I don't know why I was so certain it was true. "Kept a little product for yourself to get through this. The boyfriend knows you're a user. A drug overdose would let Jon deliver Marley to them." I went over it, trying to face the horrible truth. "Your boyfriend knows you well enough to
218

believe that you would overdo it with all that stuff right there at your disposal. Your dead body and some of his property would have done the trick. They wouldn't have killed Jon. There would have been no need to," I took my time thinking it through, "and if you died and then Jon turned up dead it would have alerted the police there was more than a drug overdose happening." I studied her. "You knew what Jon was going to do."

She tilted her head to glance up at me warily, as if she knew how close to the edge of reason I was. She whispered, "We couldn't do anything else."

"You could have tried giving the drugs back."

"Jon wanted me to." She shook her head in denial. "This was my only chance at a new life. I need that money. I'm going to have plastic surgery, move to LA and start over Besides, you don't steal from Giovanni and walk away. He'd take the drugs and still kill me."

"Is Marley still alive?" It was a hard question to ask.

She shrugged. "As far as I know."

"Would Jon tell you if he'd killed her?"

She didn't answer, which was an answer in itself. "He must have told you something about where he hid her."

"Like I said, the less he told me the safer he felt. I didn't care about any of the details. I just wanted to get out of here and start over."

"Well, you're not going to be starting over." I had to go on believing that Marley was still alive and that we could find her. "You're going to give me the drugs so we can buy Marley back."

"Like shit." The words of denial exploded out of her.

I hit her with my closed fist. It knocked her sideways but the look she gave me said it wasn't the first fist she'd known and she wasn't really impressed, so I hit her again. Her head jerked back but that was just about the only reaction I got from her.

"Wait!" Lexi got between us. "Maybe we don't need the drugs; we only need to pretend to have them. Maybe that will be enough to get Marley back."

"They aren't going to give her up without the goods. This is real life, Lexi, not television."

"It's worth a try." She turned her back to me and faced Jodi. "Where are these guys? How do we get in touch with them?"

Jodi shrugged and cupped her cheek. "I don't know where they are."

"They're here somewhere in Key West," I said. "We need to find those guys before I can make the exchange."

Blood dripped from her lip. She tasted it with her tongue and then she said, "You don't get it, do you? With or without the drugs, they'll never let me walk away alive. You don't steal from them without retribution. They'll take everything and kill her anyway. There's no buying your way out of this situation."

"Do they have Marley already?"

"I don't know."

"Why would they kill Jon if they didn't have her?"

"I don't know that either. Something must have gone wrong."

"You think?"

"Even if they have her, if they don't realize she's the wrong woman, she should be safe for a bit." And then she added. "At least until they find the drugs."

I paced around the small motel room. "And then what? What happens to Marley after they decide they've got the wrong woman?"

She shrugged. She had no more guilt or worry over the pain she'd caused than she would have over killing a fly. "They want the drugs."

"Which you have."

"No, Jon has them. Or had them. He was going to sell them."

"How was he going to do that?"

"There's a guy on the island here who has connections in Miami."

I had a good idea who that might be. But did I believe that she would have handed over the drugs to Jon? Just how much did these siblings trust one another? And where could Jodi hide the drugs in this small place? I paced the room, watching to see if she reacted when I got close to any particular spot. Nothing showed on her face, but then I already knew she was a good actress. I asked, "What makes you think Jon hadn't already sold the drugs before he was killed?"

She sat up ramrod straight. "He would have said."

"Unless he intended to sell them and leave you behind."

"He wouldn't do that to me!"

"Yeah? Why do you think the coke isn't here with you?"

She jumped to her feet, all her cool control gone. I pushed her back down, sending the chair skidding backwards under her. "He was packed and about to leave town when he was killed." Jodi's eyes narrowed into suspicious slits. I had her full attention now, so I added, "And he'd already sold the drugs."

She gulped air.

"He didn't tell you that, did he?"

She shook her head. "Was he going to screw me out of my share?" It came out as a whimper.

"He didn't come for you, did he?" Her shoulders slumped in despair. My cruel words had hurt her more than my hands had. "Why would he share with you when he could have it all for himself?"

"The bastard!" she yelled, and then she began to cry while she cursed him.

"Shut up," I bellowed. She stopped swearing and watched me intently, knowing more was coming. "Jon has a girlfriend here. What's her name?"

"He never mentioned her. Is she in on this?"

"You know your brother better than anyone. Would he cut somebody else in?"

Her face contorted into an angry mask of hatred. "Bastard," she said again. "Was she going with Jon?" Tears rolled down her cheeks.

If Jon's girlfriend was holding Marley, Jodi knew nothing about it. "What about Simon, was he in on it?" I asked.

"Who?" Her face was blank confusion. "Does that guy have my money?" She scrambled to her feet. "Where is he? I want my money."

If Simon was holding Marley, Jodi knew nothing about it. She was focused on me, and ready to go along with anyone who could help her to get out of this. More than that, she still hoped to get the money. "What are you going to do?" she asked in a small voice.

It was a good question. Jodi watched me intently. Could she tell me anything else? And how much of her story was true? "Lexi, do you mind staying here with her until the police come?"

Jodi yelped and shot toward me, ready to use her nails, but Lexi pushed her back into the chair. "I'll wait here," Lexi said, "but what are you going to do?"

"Not sure."

"Yes, you are."

"I'm not going to do anything crazy."

"Shit." Lexi was not buying my vagueness. "Don't do it, Sherri. I don't even know what it is but I know you shouldn't do it."

I handed her McPhee's card. "Call the cops."

Chapter 32

It had started to rain. The windshield wipers could barely keep up.

I quickly backed the jeep out of the lane, wanting to be well away before McPhee showed up. As I drove, by instinct rather than consciously and without a destination in mind, I focused on Jodi's story, trying to find something, anything that I'd missed, some clue to finding Marley. The problem was that Jon hadn't shared his plan with his sister — if he'd had a plan at all. My guess was he'd made it up as he went along.

It had been chance that Jon knew Jodi's doppelganger was visiting Lexi, too good a chance to pass up. If Jodi hadn't been in trouble it would have been an interesting coincidence and nothing more, but Jon had been handed a substitute for his sister. It wasn't love at first sight that had him so excited — it was millions of dollars of drug money. Where had he hidden those drugs? I hadn't seen any sign of them in the house, although I hadn't been searching for them. I was guessing that Jon wouldn't want to leave them in his place. He wouldn't want to make it easy on anyone hunting for them. Had he hired a lockup somewhere or were they in the same place he'd put Marley?

I'd been driving in a daze with no idea what came next or where I was going. Now I realized I was passing Rude

George's. It looked closed. The only connections Jon seemed to have in Key West were Simon and an unknown girlfriend, an older woman Simon hadn't met. There must be some way to find her, some small thing to help identify her. Maybe the key in my pocket was to something of the girlfriend's. A padlocked shed was my guess. I looked up at the sky, checking the weather. Not much time left. If I didn't find Marley in the next few hours...

I needed to find the girlfriend and Simon was the only one who had mentioned her. I pulled over, the right front wheel scraping the curb and the rear end barely out of traffic. There was an old yellow slicker on the back seat. I pulled it on and jogged back to the restaurant. The steel barriers were down but the door was still open. An iron wall of metal had closed over the outdoor bar and the staff were stacking the last of the chairs in the kitchen.

Gary, hustling to the kitchen with a load of chairs, told me Simon had already left and he didn't give out information on his staff. Men hate a crying woman. It was the only remaining weapon I had. It got messy before he told me how to find Simon. "He may have left town already," Gary said. "Selfish bastard wouldn't even stay a half-hour to help finish up."

Through the rain, I could see the little cottage at the back of an attractive two-storied white house that had been boarded up against the storm. I ran for the gate. Water was already pooling on the walkway.

226

I stepped out of the weather onto the tiny porch of the cottage and knocked. After a few minutes, I pounded some more, huddling close to the building for shelter. Nobody came. Perhaps he had already left. I leaned over the railing to look in the window and caught Simon, wearing only red boxers, peeking out to see who was at the door. I gave him a big smile and a cheerful wave.

The first thing he said when he opened the door was, "I'm busy. I can't talk to you." He tried to shut the door but my foot was already blocking it. "Of course, you are. Everyone is leaving." But I was pretty sure I hadn't disturbed his packing.

"Go away."

"Please," I begged. "I only need a minute."

"Go away."

"Talk to me or talk to the cops."

Now I had his attention. He looked over his shoulder at the bedroom door. "Look," I said. "I'm not trying to jam you up, I just want to find Marley. What if Jon locked her somewhere in this heat with no food or water and Alma coming? If he's the only one who knew where she is..." I couldn't finish the sentence.

"It's not my problem."

"It will be if you know where she is and don't say anything. You'll be responsible for what happens. If she dies, you'll have murdered her."

Panic showed on his face. "I don't know anything about what Jon did."

"Talking to me will only take a minute. The police will take longer."

He frowned. Staying off the radar was important to this guy. He raised his shoulders and his hands. "Look, I have no idea what Jon was up to and I don't know where your friend is."

"Please, let me in. I only want a minute."

I thought he was going to push me away but finally he stepped back, deciding I'd give him less hassle than the police. Inside, I had a good look around. What had once been a pool cabana was now partitioned into two rooms, what I guessed was a bedroom, and the living space we were in. If he was hiding drugs or Marley it had to be in the bedroom. The way he glanced at that door said something in there was making him nervous. I wanted to see what it was.

"This has nothing to do with me," he said. "So why don't you just go ask your questions somewhere else."

Maybe my success with Gary was bringing out my dramatic side. I collapsed onto the floor and started bawling. It wasn't hard.

Simon bent toward me, hands on his knees, and spoke clearly and loudly as though my crying like a baby had inhibited my ability to understand language. "I don't know anything about this business. Jon never told me anything about any of this. We weren't that close." He jerked upright and went to the kitchenette.

From the bedroom behind him a girl stepped into the room. Barefoot, she wore tiny black shorts and a white peasant top that fell off one bare shoulder. With long blond hair and a gorgeous body, she looked like a swimsuit model, but if she was eighteen, I was the queen of Siam. I could rule out Simon as the person holding Marley.

She leaned against the door-jamb and placed her left foot on her right calf. "You should help her, Simon."

His cheeks flushed with anger. "Go back in and close the door."

When the door closed behind her I said, "She's underage."

"It's none of your business."

"Hmmmm…" I waited a beat and then added. "Maybe not my business, but definitely police business."

"What do you want?"

"I need to know about that woman he was seeing."

"I told you everything I know about her."

"Seriously, Dude," I said, using his own words. I glanced at the bedroom door again. "Everything?"

"Everything!"

Beside me the television was playing softly, a Miami station warning that all residents should evacuate Key West immediately. *Not yet.* It was the one thing that was clear to me. *I can't leave yet.*

"Here," he said. I took the glass of water he held out. "There might be something you forgot." I sipped the water. "Do you know where he met her?"

"No. He already knew her last year when he played here."

"So, you knew Jon last year?" I took another sip of water.

"Yes."

"But you never met her?"

"Didn't I just say that?" He gave a cocky little smile. "He was too smart to introduce me to his meal ticket."

I nodded in understanding. "Couldn't stand the competition, right?"

"Right." He took the glass out of my hand. "Now go!"

I climbed to my feet but I wasn't quite finished with Simon. "How did he describe her?"

"He just said she was generous with her gifts and not too hard to please, but it helped if he kept his eyes shut." He laughed, not a pleasant sound. He put his hand on my arm, pushing me to the door.

"So, you never ran into them anywhere and he never said her name?"

"No." And then he frowned. I waited, standing close enough to him to smell his Polo aftershave, while he chased a memory.

He tilted his head concentrating. "He just called her Lena, yeah, that was it, Lena." He smiled, pleased with himself. "But her name won't help you. Jon told me she left for Europe just after he arrived here. He tried to talk her into taking him along." Simon laughed. "He didn't have a hope. From what he told me, she out-classed him like crazy, a society woman with lots of cash."

"Do you know any other friends of his?"

"Nope, but he told me once that he was born here and spent the first four years of his life in Key West before he moved to Atlanta. But it's not likely he knows anyone here now."

"If you remember anything else, will you call me?" I pulled one of the Sunset's business cards from my wallet and handed it to him.

"I won't remember anything more. You know everything I do."

"Still…"

He opened the door and stood there holding it, waiting for me to leave. I nodded at the bedroom. "You should get her to a shelter."

"Mind your own business."

I headed back to the jeep. The weather was worsening by the minute and I had run out of time. I needed to return's Petra's ride in case she changed her mind about leaving.

At the house Petra had been working hard. All the hanging plants had been stripped from the yard and the wicker furniture was gone from the porch.

When Petra opened the door, I held out her car keys. "No luck," she said. It was a statement, not a question. "What will you do now?"

"I can't think of anywhere else to look. I guess now I wait."

"In Key West or back in Jacaranda?"

"I'm staying here."

She nodded. "This old house will keep you safe. Where's Lexi?"

"At the Rawhide. She's keeping it open until the last moment, having a big hurricane party."

"Don't let her stay there too long. That place won't hold. You both get yourselves back here before long, you hear?"

"Yes, ma'am."

There was no line up at the Rawhide, no one sitting on the porch with their feet up on the railing and a drink in their hand. Inside, the few drinkers remaining behind instead of evacuating were having a party, determined to enjoy themselves. There's always one bar in town that stays open to accommodate the stupid few.

232

In my hometown, it's Junior's. Those of us who leave always call Junior's to see how the storm is progressing. If they didn't answer we'd know things had gone terribly wrong and it would be a long time before we could return.

Lexi came out from behind the bar when she saw me. "Is Tanya here?" I asked. "I want to avoid her." She may be undercover but there was nothing to prevent her from calling McPhee and telling her where to find me.

Lexi looked around the room. "No," she replied. "But she may come in. You can wait in the office."

Lexi unlocked the office door, saying, "Where have you been and why haven't you answered your phone?"

"I turned it off. It needs charging." She held out her hand and I gave it to her. I watched her plug it in and said, "I know the name of the woman Jon was seeing."

Lexi's sequined shorts were draped over the chair behind the tiny desk. She must have come directly to the Rawhide from Jodi's motel and changed clothes in the office.

Lexi asked, "Where have you been and what have you been doing?"

I gave her a one line update. My voice was hoarse with tiredness, so tired I almost couldn't get the words out.

Lexi wrinkled her nose. "You don't smell good."

"It's hot out there and I spilled coffee on myself earlier." I pulled my shirt out from my body and had a good look at it. "I was wearing this tee yesterday."

233

"It smells like it."

I lifted my arm and sniffed. She was right, I reeked.

"Girl, there's no need to feel bad and look bad too." She started picking through the boxes stacked against the wall. She opened a box and found what she wanted. She threw a black tee shirt at me. It had a white outline of Papa Hemingway on it. "It's from Hemingway Days last year." She pointed to a closed door on the back wall. "Wash up a bit and change your shirt while I get you something to eat."

I pulled my shirt off and let it drop to the floor. "I haven't got time."

"Yes, you have." She pointed at me. "Look at yourself. You're exhausted. And when did you last eat?"

I stood there with the black shirt in my hand and considered her question. Before I came up with an answer Lexi said, "Pastries and coffee for breakfast." She pointed to the door. "Get in there and wash, and don't put on that shirt until you do. Some of my staff bailed, leaving ahead of the storm. I'll be waiting tables and seating the customers and working the bar. Stupid idea to stay open. Another hour and I'm closing it down." Frazzled and worn out, her make-up was faded and her hair disheveled. This weekend was taking its toll on both of us, but she'd taken time to dress in a sparkly black sheath and dangerously high heels. "I'll bring you something, you look like you're totally done."

She was right. I was on the point of collapse. I went into the powder room and looked in the mirror. Despair had painted itself on my face. Black circles under my eyes, no makeup except flecks of yesterday's mascara on my cheeks, and my hair… well, let's just say any decent hairdresser would weep at the sight. I'd basically slept in my clothes the night before. I wasn't a pretty sight.

I tidied up, washing with rough paper towels and combing my hair. Nothing to be done with my haggard face, grim with desolation, but at least I wouldn't frighten strangers now. With time running out, my horror was already turning into loss, dragging my features down and taking any spark of life from my face. I turned out the light, unable to bear what was staring back at me, a person who had given up and had no place to turn.

Chapter 33

Lexi returned with a sandwich and a coffee as I shut the door to the powder room. "I'd have brought you a real meal but I know you wouldn't have eaten it."

I wasn't sure I could choke this down. Lexi accurately read my face. She set the sandwich on the cluttered desk and said, "You have to try. You're about ready to pass out. You're no good to Marl if you can't walk."

"Alma is moving faster than they said."

"I know. I can see it out there."

"What in hell does it mean to Marley?"

"It means we have to hurry."

She moved aside a stack of invoices and set the coffee down. "Eat first and then we'll talk about what comes next."

I slumped down onto the rolling office chair. I was out of steam and out of hope and eating had become a harsh necessity. "Tell me what happened with Jodi and the cops."

"Confusing! McPhee somehow got the idea she was coming to pick up Jon's sister and you."

"I wonder where she got that idea."

She grinned. "She was much more interested in you than in Jodi."

"She must have been very disappointed at my absence."

"Not to mention annoyed."

"What else?"

"Not much. Jodi is accusing you of assault and wants charges brought. McPhee seems to agree."

"Lovely! Assault and murder, McPhee must be looking forward to some quality time with me. No mention of theft?"

"The key didn't come into the discussion."

This made me smile and I saw the beam of delight that lit Lexi's face. Poor McPhee: losing evidence to a suspect must hurt like hell.

I told Lexi about Simon. "I have no idea how to find Jon's girlfriend. Do you know anyone named Lena? She's older than Jon, so in her fifties, quite well off and probably in Europe."

"Doesn't ring my bell but I'll ask around and put it out on social media." Lexi stood up. "Something will turn up."

Did she really believe that? I wished I did.

When the door closed behind her I realized that I hadn't thanked her for organizing a search and putting up posters. It had turned up more information than all my running around and trouble. In the end, I probably hadn't improved Marley's chances of being found. That realization did nothing to raise my spirits.

I took a bite of the sandwich, but it was no use. I might need the fuel but my throat just closed around it when I tried to swallow. I pushed away from the desk.

Out in the hall, music was playing loud enough to drown out the wind. Willie Nelson sang about blue skies. I stopped. The song grabbed me, cutting into my heart which was already on the edge of breaking. At that moment, blue skies sounded like the saddest thing in the world, an impossible wish. All Willie's bad days might be gone, but if Marley didn't come back, mine would never end. Tears blurred my sight. I'd been distraught and shattered by losing Clay, wasn't near able to cope with the sorrow, and now... I leaned back against the wall and took deep slow breaths to fight down the panic overwhelming me.

Dix stepped into the hall, looking over his shoulder toward the bar as he came. He stopped, his back to me, watching the saloon. He had his phone to his ear. He said, "He's here. Come in now." He slapped his phone shut, and then some sixth sense made him turn around. He frowned. I could see his first impulse, an instinct to destroy me, flash across his face. Color swelled up his neck.

My trailer park survival instinct kicked in. I swayed my way toward him. "Hey, big guy," I said. "I'm out of here. Want to join me?" I looked as fetching as a rash but that wouldn't slow down a guy like Dix. He'd hungrily take a bite out of anything on the table.

Suspicious and worried, he tilted his head to the side and studied me. I didn't like that look.

"Let's have a little fun." Serious stuff was going on. I could tell by the way he frowned he was still perturbed over what I might have heard and how it affected him. He was asking his reptilian brain if I was going to be a witness for the prosecution.

238

"Come on," I urged. "You're always up for a good time. And I'm a very good time."

His eyes narrowed. "Did you find Marley?"

"Naw, I guess she decided to leave without me. She'll be in touch. But now I'm looking for someone to ride out the storm with." My rocking hips underlined the image.

He grinned. His libido had always been stronger than his brain power. "Can't." Regret etched his face. "Wish I could."

"Leave early. I'll square it with Lexi." I tried to give him a smile. "Come on."

"Damn, I want to but..." He gave a little fatalistic lift of his shoulders. Dix was up to something real nasty if he didn't want what was being offered.

"Aah," I nodded my head in pretend understanding. "Another date."

He relaxed now. I was no threat to him. He grinned. "I wish. But even if I had another date I'd cancel it for you. I just need to stay here for a little while. Some guys are coming by. I need to see them. Why don't we get together in a couple of hours?"

I shook my head. "Now or never, it's a limited time offer."

"Don't do this to me. I'll collect my dough and we'll hightail it up to Miami and have us a time."

I laughed and walked off, skirting his hands that were reaching out for me.

239

My mind was doing somersaults as I searched the room, trying to figure out what was going to happen. Dix had been looking back into the saloon, checking on someone while he spoke on his cell. Lexi was talking to father Pat and that's where Dix's attention had been focused. Was Lexi in trouble? And if so, what kind? But had it been Lexi or the priest Dix was talking about? It could be someone I didn't even know. And who was Dix telling to come in? I didn't have long to wonder. Even before I had decided whether to hang in for Lexi's sake or get out of there for Marley's, trouble arrived.

Chapter 34

There were three of them. Two of them still wore riding masks up over their noses like bandits. Dressed in leather from their heavy kick-ass boots to their leather riding chaps and vests, they were evil walking.

The arrival of the three bikers tainted the air like a malevolent aroma. Saying nothing, just remaining still and watching, they awoke fear even in those who were beyond caution and too drunk to reason. The mood altered in the flicker of an eyelash. Everyone in the room felt the change from the best of times to the worst. Rustling uneasily, and stealing glances toward the bikers, people picked up their drinks and eased away from trouble. The three guys in black stood there motionless, like they owned the place and were checking out their assets. The guy in the center, the one without a mask, was clearly the one in charge. Built like a fire plug, every inch of his exposed skin had a tat on it, including a giant thunderbolt on his cheek. When he turned around to check out the two laughing guys entering the bar behind him, I saw a huge confederate flag stitched on the leather across his back. The new arrivals stopped, took in the death riders, and backed away, moving closer to each other for comfort or protection, while trying to decide if they would turn and run or skirt the darkness before them and scurry for the safety of the other humans bunched together near the stage.

I darted down the bar to Tanya. "Check out what just came in."

"I already saw them." She didn't turn to look at them, while I hadn't taken my eyes off them. "The storm is bringing all kinds of rats out of their hiding places," she said. "Coming out in the light to take advantage of the cover that Alma gives them."

"That bunch are trouble walking," I told her.

The big guy felt me watching him and locked his eyes on mine. I ducked my head, swallowed hard, and whispered, "I once saw guys from that gang down in Everglades City. They trashed a place because the fries that came with the burgers were cold. The owner was too afraid to call the cops."

She pushed her drink away. "Fear is why the Strikers stay in business. There's only about thirty in the club but they're the most violent band in all Florida. The big guy in the middle is called 'The Hammer.' His real name is Terry Bosch." She still hadn't looked their way, but she was keeping track of events in the mirror. "He's the head of the Strikers, as mean a bastard as you'll ever see."

"Charming."

"Oh yeah. They're all white racists and anti-Semitics. They bring in most of the meth that enters Miami."

"Are you from Miami?"

She went on speaking like I hadn't even asked the question. "One of the others is probably Marshall Towes, The

242

Hammer's bum wipe. Terry never goes anywhere without him. No telling who the other one is."

"Will they recognize you?"

"Unlikely, I was in a patrol car in Tampa the last time I met up with them. I'm on loan to the special operations here in Key West. Maybe Terry and his friends just came in for a drink. Maybe they're nothing to worry about."

"Yeah and maybe the sun really does shine out my ass. They don't look like they came in for a bit of fun, at least not the kind the rest of the lunatics are looking for." A man, watching the bikers, bumped into me. I pushed him away and he muttered "Sorry" as he stumbled on.

"I heard Dix, the bartender, talking on his cell." I repeated the conversation. "He's here," that's what he said. Dix was looking at Lexi and Father Pat. I don't know which one of them he was talking about, but it was one of them, and then the bikers walked in. I don't want anything to happen to Lexi."

"She's okay."

"It's Father Pat you're after, isn't it? He's selling opioids."

Tanya head shot up. "You sound like a cop."

"Nope, just a bartender with lots of experience of the wrong kind. Why are the Strikers here?"

"Maybe they're going to branch out from meth and they're trying to muscle in on Pat's business. We're trying to

243

find his pipeline. It would be worth a lot of money to the Strikers."

Shoulder to shoulder in a solid line, the three guys walked to the bar. Near the bar, one man, less aware than other people, looked up to see them and jumped back, saying "Holy shit." They just kept walking.

Tanya had her cell out.

"Are you calling for backup?"

"Damn right." She frowned as she peered at her screen. "Can't call from here, it's a dead zone."

"Dix got a connection."

"Well, I can't."

"Go into the office. There's a land line."

"First, I'm going to go get those two," Tanya said, and nodded in the direction of Lexi and Father Pat. "Take them with me. You go and wait in the office for us."

"Look, I don't want to get involved with this. Those guys scare the life out of me."

"Go," she said. Tanya didn't care about my feelings.

Chapter 35

In the office, Tanya pointed from Lexi to the priest and said, "Those bikers out there are here for one of you."

"Not me." Lexi protested. "I never saw them before."

"You sure you haven't ticked someone off?" Tanya raised her hand to stop Lexi as she started to defend herself. "It has to be one of you."

Lexi cursed her denial.

"Lexi, we both know you can go off on people without a lot of cause," I put in. "Besides your great clothes you're known for your," I searched for a word... "irritability."

For once, Lexi held her temper. "I promise they have no reason to come for me."

Pat washed his hands in apprehension. "It may be me." He looked ill.

"Why?" Lexi asked, truly baffled.

Neither Tanya nor the priest jumped in to enlighten her, so I did. "Pat is running a drugstore out of your bar, running it out of bars up and down Duval, but mostly here. His customers just wait for him to come by every night with their little feel-good pills."

"I don't believe it," Lexi said.

Hadn't I told her that Pat was a drug dealer? Amazing what we can ignore when we don't want to listen.

Tanya, at the desk punching in numbers, said without looking up, "It's true. If you checked the inside pockets of his priestly black jacket you'd find all kinds of little baggies full of stuff." She pointed at the desk. "And by the way, I want them right here, now." She tapped the scarred wood in front of her. Pat hesitated but then he reached inside his jacket and started to pull out small clear bags of pills while Lexi cursed him in rich and colorful language.

Tanya said, "How could this come as a surprise to you? He wasn't exactly subtle."

"Lexi's an innocent despite her shiny veneer," I said, coming to her defense. I parked my ass on the edge of the desk. "Besides, there always people selling things in bars – drugs, sex, used cars, just recently a guy tried to sell me a horse, why he thought I'd need a horse I can't guess." My mouth just keeps running when I'm nervous. I crossed my arms, trying for a casualness I wasn't feeling, while my foot was going up and down like a metronome on speed.

"But I know he's helped people," Lexi protested.

"Sure, it's part of his cover. Pat came in singing a sad song to tug at your heart and make you like him. Great story, still administering to his flock even though he'd been turfed out of the cloister. Only he's been administering something besides goodness and light to his parishioners. First night here, I got a peek in the men's room and saw him exchange a baggy for cash.

But he's using his own stuff and he's getting careless. Even the priestly act isn't going to save him."

"You son of a bitch." Lexi's hands came off her hips and curled into fists.

"What's the big deal?" Pat said. "It was only a few pills."

"I don't want any shit associated with my bar. Everyone knows I run a decent spot, an honest place. I'm going to make you so sorry." Pat backed into the corner away from her.

"Geez, Lexi," I said, "you've still got too much testosterone. Chill."

Tanya hung up the phone. Her face was worried.

"What?" I asked.

"There's a problem down by the beach. All the street crime units and every cruiser the force owns is down there sorting it out. A riot or fight has broken out. I have to take Pat out on my own." She looked around. "Is there some way I can get him out of here without going back out there?"

Lexi shook her head. "Just through the kitchen or out the front door. To go through the kitchen, we have to go out to the bar." She looked up at the window behind Tanya. "But there's always the window."

I was betting Lexi had exited lots of joints that way — and she'd probably done it wearing high heels.

Tanya frowned and then shook her head. "I'll take him out the front. I just hope there aren't any more bikers waiting outside for us."

"Don't be a fool." I stood up. "There's three of them and one of you."

"And it's three miles to the station," Lexi put in as she went to the door and turned the door knob to lock us in. "Lots can happen before you get there. Stay here and wait it out until help comes."

"By the time they break up the crowd down at the beach," she paced behind the desk, thinking it through, "it might be an hour or more. I'm not waiting."

That's when I had my bright idea. The office also functioned as a storage room for supplies and costumes. I pulled a purple wrap off a hanger. "Let's see how Pat would look as a middle-aged woman from upper New York, say Saratoga." I pulled at his shirt. "Take this off. And that jacket. And lose the cross."

"What?" He looked as shocked as if I'd told him to get naked so I could ravish him.

"The jacket, take it off." I was already searching through a pile of costumes hanging from a coat rack for something to fit his bottom half. "What have you got that will fit him, Lexi?"

She studied him dubiously for a moment and then pulled out a length of flowing Hawaiian print. She fastened it around

248

his waist and knotted it at his hip and then she took a blond wig out of a box and settled it on his head. She stood back and looked at him critically. "You weren't much as a man, but you sure as hell make one ugly woman." She finger-combed the wig into a chin length bob and smoothed down the bangs.

"That's never going to fool anyone," Tanya said.

"Well, not on its own, but if Lexi and I create a little diversion you may be able to sneak him out."

"I'm not sure," Tanya said, worrying her bottom lip.

"Got a better idea?"

"Nope."

"If this fails you won't be any worse off."

She wasn't buying it.

"Want to go it alone? Go out there with guns blazing!"

"Hell, no."

I grinned at Lexi. "Got your dancing shoes on, Lexi? I did it alone last time." I wrapped a white feather boa around my shoulders. "Tonight, it's a sister act. Shall we show them how the girls get it done?"

Lexi wasn't happy. "This is a bad idea."

"Well, here's the thing. Either Pat dies, and maybe Tanya too, or you and I make fools of ourselves. You choose."

"Well, if you put it that way." She actually grinned. "If you're up for it, so am I, but I hate to think what it will do to my reputation." She threw back her head with laughter.

"It's not as though it will be the first time…making fools of ourselves." I held out a second boa, pink this time, and grinned back at Lexi. "Besides," I said, "We both learned long ago that a little embarrassment isn't fatal."

Chapter 36

A phone rang, jangling our nerves. For a minute, we all froze in shock and looked at each other. "It's mine," Pat finally said. He held his cell as if it were in imminent danger of exploding, his, "Hello," tentative and uncertain. As he listened, his face went pale. It was a long call, but Pat didn't say anything. He hit End and said, "That was Maria, telling me her son, Joseph, is dead." Pat was crying. Huge snuffles of distress seeped from him. "He was out making deliveries when he was taken. She got a call. Some man on the phone told her that her son was dead but she was still in business, only now she's working for them. When she asked what they'd done to her son, they said that he had been struck by lightning. And then they laughed." Pat was shaking. Sweat glistened on his face and bald head.

"The Strikers," Tanya said. She pulled out the chair from behind the desk and took it to him, guiding him down onto it. "Did he tell her anything else?" Tanya asked.

"They told her I was out, that they had a new distributor in Key West. When Joseph made his first communion, I was there." He sobbed, lowering his head onto his hands as though he could hold back the pain.

"So, you're responsible for getting him killed." Tanya's voice was as harsh as her words. "You got him into this."

"No," he wailed and shook his head in denial. "I was only trying to help. Maria's husband had a supply line to Mexico. He started selling pills into biker territory without permission. He disappeared, but the pills kept on coming, piling up, so I started a little dial-a-drug business to help the family. We weren't hurting anyone."

"Why did you come down to Key West?" Tanya asked. "Because it was safer here?"

"It was open territory. I didn't want to compete with the Strikers. I sold from Homestead on down south. I only go up to Miami once a week when a shipment arrives. I pick up the pills and then I get out of there." He looked from one of us to the other. "It's not like I'm selling hard drugs. These actually help people."

"Don't give me that shit. They help you," Tanya said. Her voice had lost its warm drawl.

Pat wasn't done defending himself. He said, "I've poured lots of wine over eager lips with the Pope's blessing, a little chemical doesn't hurt." He turned away from Tanya and reached out a pleading hand to Lexi, hoping for an ally. "Look, people come through your door to find me. I bring in business."

"I don't want your kind of business. You're a parasite."

He sneered. "A lady with a chorus line of beautiful bare-bottomed boys passing judgment on me." He made the sign of the cross in the air.

"Cut the shit and get out of here before I break a few of your bones." She pointed to the door. "Go."

He licked his lips. "Maria said they were coming for me, told me to run for my life."

Lexi shook out her feathers. "But first we got to dance for your life. I'm not sure you're worth it." She unlocked the door. "Come on, Sherri."

We were all guts and glory when we went through the door but our bravado came to an abrupt end when we saw what was waiting for us. The three bikers formed a wall in front of us. "Oh shit." I heard the click of the door locking behind us.

Lexi's brain was quicker than mine. She slinked toward them, her hips rolling like the surf. "Don't leave before you see the show, boys. It'll get your engines started." She rubbed her pink feathers across The Hammer's face. "I'll put a little extra in it for you, big guy."

He batted her hand away. "Get lost, you mutant."

This was a really, really, really, bad thing to say to Lexi. If he'd only asked, I would have told him but he was already heading for the office door. When he couldn't open it, it only took him one kick to splinter the wood. The knob, surrounded by shattered wood, was still there but the rest was on the floor. I could hear Pat squealing like a baby from inside the darkened office.

The Hammer started to step over the kindling to get into the office. The light went on. Tanya, holding a gun with both hands straight out towards The Hammer, yelled, "Stop, Police!" She might just as well have said, "Save me, Jesus," for all the good it did. One biker, walking slightly ahead of the other two, lunged sideways into the office. There was a gunshot followed by a scream.

The Hammer had no intention of backing off. He stepped onto the door as Lexi stomped forward and roared, "Wait one God damn minute."

He turned to look at her, raising his fist, probably intending to drive it straight into her face, but he was too slow — or maybe he just didn't take Lexi seriously. He should have. Her skirt was up to her waist. With her weight on her left foot, her right shot out from the hip like a pile driver with a stiletto on the end of it. Terry Bosch's face exploded into a red mask and he staggered backwards into the office. Lexi kicked him again before he hit the floor. The third guy, The Hammer's pet, backed up against the wall with his hands over his head, yelling, "I haven't done anything."

Behind me I heard, "What the hell?" Dix had arrived. He pulled something out of his back pocket and rushed toward Lexi, who was still concentrating on The Hammer.

Chapter 37

Not to be left entirely out of the fun, I kicked sideways at Dix's left knee just like Tully had taught me. There was a satisfying scream of pain from him as he crumpled. But he wasn't done. He was already raising his hand with the leather sap in it when my heel smashed into his face, driving him sideways into the wall. I stomped him hard in another delicate place for all the times he'd taken advantage, and then I reached out for the weapon that had fallen from his hand. I tapped it against my palm, testing it. Unlike a Billy-club, this was flat. Weighted with lead, it's called a beavertail and it's a lovely weapon, designed to hit hard and take your opponent out. Lots of bartenders and bouncers carry them, and I'd always wanted one of my own. When I asked Tully to get me one, he said, "It'll only get you in trouble." He meant that it would give me a false sense of confidence.

Now I had one. I brought it down on Dix's shoulder, just to get the feel of it, and then slid it into my back pocket and pulled my Hemingway shirt down over it. "Thanks, Dix," I said. "I'll treasure it always." Dix was screaming in pain and didn't care about my gratitude.

Lexi was still waiting to see if the guy with his hands in the air was going to behave but she gave me a glance over her shoulder. "You okay?" she asked.

"Yup." It was true. Adrenalin was pumping and I felt better than I had in months as I listened to Tanya read someone their rights.

The Hammer moaned, but he wasn't going anywhere.

I pointed down at him and said, "Nice one, Lexi."

She patted her hair into place and straightened her gown at the bust. "When you grow up a girl in a guy's body, you need to know how to look after yourself if you ever want to turn into a woman." She smoothed down her skirt. "And baby, I turned into a woman." She gave a little growl and waggled her hips as she made her way down the hall. The noise had brought onlookers in twos and threes, peering around the corner. If the situation got out of control they were ready to dart to safety like a school of chum when a barracuda shows up. At the same time, they didn't want to miss out on the action. Raising her arms to crowd them away in front of her, Lexi moved forward and said, "The excitement's over, folks. It's time for everyone to have a free drink. Set 'em up boys. Give the customers a drink on the house." She made a circle with her finger, signaling for the hoedown and setting the waiters to yipping and yelling and running for the stage.

It wasn't over yet. A surprising amount of blood was still flowing. The Hammer's face was sliced from his lip to his eye by Lexi's dangerous heel. Dix's teeth and his nose gushed gobs of blood. His groin, shoulder and knee... well, at least they didn't bleed, but it would be some time before he went dancing. Tanya had shot one of the Strikers in the shoulder. Ambulances, police and statements were yet to come. It would take forever. I didn't have forever.

Tanya was cuffing the third Striker when she saw me heading for the door. "Where do you think you're going?" Tanya, no longer the hooker with a heart, stared at me with flinty cop eyes, a cop who had everything under control.

"Just need some fresh air."

"And I need you to stay here."

I grinned at her. "What are you going to do if I leave, shoot me?"

"I might." Surrounded by villains and blood, we both knew she was already well in over her head. "I need your statement."

"You'll get it." I headed for the door.

"Sherri."

I kept moving, walking backward to the door and barely slowing down, but wanting to hear what she had to say.

"We found your friend's purse and ID at Jodi's apartment. There's now an APB out for Marley. We're looking."

I stopped walking. "Jodi Kidd was going to use Marley's identity, go west and start over. That's what she told me."

She nodded. "Looks like that was their plan."

We both knew there was more to what they were planning. "If they had her identity, why keep Marley alive? Jon was going to make Marley's death look like a drug overdose and then he was going to plant Jodi's papers on her body, passing Marley off as Jodi to stop Giovanni from looking for her."

"That's what we think. The two guys that came from Miami to collect Jodi have only seen her picture."

Was Marley already dead? More than ever, I needed to keep looking.

Tanya said, "There is some good news, we got one of the guys who killed Jon." She grinned. "Driving around a small town in a rental with a trunk that won't close kind of makes you stand out. Seems the night Jon died, the perp drove around and around for over an hour. Someone took down the license plate number and turned it over to us when we did our house to house. We picked him up this morning"

"That's good, but why did they kill Jon?"

"Basically, it seems things got out of control. We haven't sorted it yet but the guy is claiming self-defense."

"So, McPhee knows I had nothing to do with Jon's death?" Relief, but not much.

"She knows." She frowned. "She's still not happy with you, told me to bring you in. Why is that?"

"No idea." My hand went to the key still hidden in my pocket, checking that it was still there. It had become a talisman for me, a lucky charm.

"Well, there's a second guy and he's still on the loose. Keep your head down until we get him."

"Sure."

"What does that mean?" she asked.

I grinned at her. "I have no idea."

"Be careful," Tanya called as the door swung closed behind me.

Chapter 38

A blast of wind nearly blew me back inside when I stepped through the door. Alma wasn't toying with us anymore. The heavy winds drove steel needles of rain into my face. It was peeing down out there. Palm trees were bent in half before the power of the wind. I leaned into the gale and left the shelter of the porch. The driving rain made it hard to breathe and I struggled to stay on my feet.

Shelter was the first order of business. But where could I find that? Most restaurants and bars were closed and shuttered. Would McPhee be waiting for me at Lexi's? She probably had better things to do, and she knew sooner or later that she'd collect me, so I headed for the apartment.

I hadn't gone one block before I knew I'd made a mistake. It wasn't just fighting the wind and the rain, it was the flying debris. Palm fronds, garbage cans, and at one point a lawn chair tumbling over and over, threatened me.

I was the only fool out there so I moved to the middle of the street, away from the trees. The rain was falling too fast for it to drain off. Already the water was accumulating on the roadbed, splashing up to my ankles. I turned a corner and now the wind was shoving me forward until I was flying ahead of it. The trip to Lexi's suddenly became a fast one.

At Petra Bishop's a security light came on, illuminating the litter covering the brick walkway. The wind pushed me before it. I grabbed the newel post at the top of the steps to slow myself down and avoid crashing through the window in the front door. The veranda was empty of furniture. I reached for my purse. That's when I remembered that everything, my key and phone included, was back on the desk at the Rawhide. "Shit." The only key I still had was the little one that I'd slipped into my right-hand pocket, the one that would open that unknown lock to free Marley.

My chest tightened with panic. I needed my phone. What if Giselle called? I wouldn't know. But it was a crazy idea anyway. No way she'd be out there working in this storm. If she hadn't left Key West she was in an emergency shelter somewhere. Lexi still had a land line in her apartment. Until I got back my cell, I was kicking it old school. I'd call Lexi and tell her to answer my cell. Now all I had to do was find a way into the house.

I stood there trying to decide how to do that, Petra opened the front door as if she'd been waiting there for me. I stumbled in, bumping into the porch furniture that now filled the entryway. There was barely a spare foot of space left to stand in. Plants sat on top of tables and chairs and even marched up the stairs, leaving only about a foot of unoccupied tread on each step.

"I just came around to see how deep the water was on the street." She was yelling over the noise of the storm, but still I could barely hear her. "Never expected to see anyone out there." She frowned. "Did you have an accident?"

The yellow slicker was back at the Rawhide. I'd walked out without it. Trying to catch my breath, I shook my head.

"Come on," she said and put her arm around my shoulders. "Let's get you upstairs and into dry clothes."

I changed and went back into the kitchen. The adrenalin rush I'd felt at the Rawhide was gone, leaving me exhausted and weak. Disappointment ate at me. There was nowhere left to search for Marley, and with the storm now raging... I'd reached the end. I had nothing left.

In the kitchen, I opened the cupboard doors searching for a drink but finding nothing. In the fridge, I found half a bottle of chardonnay. That would be a start to oblivion, the only thing I wanted at that moment.

The phone rang, a faint sound above the roar of the wind. Petra and I stared at each other in surprise. With the noise outside, it seemed like something alien.

Petra pointed to the little white princess phone hanging on the wall and said, "It's the phone," as if I didn't know.

I set the bottle on the counter and picked up the receiver. I said, "Hello," knowing it could only be more bad news, shocking and awful, for anyone to call in a raging storm.

Lexi didn't stop for niceties. "I just had a call from my friend, Suzie."

I was having trouble hearing her over the freight train sound of the wind. I pressed the phone against my ear and blocked the other one with a finger, hollering, "Speak louder."

"Suzie saw my post on Facebook. She knows who Jon's girlfriend is, a society woman called Lena who's away in Europe. Her house is empty, giving Jon a perfect place to hide Marley."

Trying to make sense, I asked, "Lena?"

"Yup."

It was almost good news. "How do I find her with just a first name?"

"That's the other part. Her name isn't Lena. It's Selena Martinez. She helps with the Pimp and Ho ball. I've never met her but Suzie went to meetings a couple of times at her place." Even at a time like this, Lexi had to give all the details.

"Would she hide a kidnapped woman for Jon?"

"Nope, but she wouldn't know. She's in Europe."

"Would the house be empty?"

"She lives alone."

"Servants?"

"Days only. Suzie said they were going to take their holidays when she went away. The staff comes back a week before Lena – a month from now."

Marley would be locked in there alone for a month. I gulped air.

"Here's her address." Lexi gave me some basic directions. "Nice part of town." She went on to give more details, but I broke in with, "Just tell me how to get there."

She did, and then added, "How will you get out there? Nothing is moving."

"I'll figure it out."

"The scooter will never get through the water. I can't come to help you."

"No problem. I'll call the police. Stay at the Rawhide."

Detective McPhee didn't answer my call, but I told her where I thought Marley would be and asked her in the strongest possible language to get her ass over there. "I'm on my way there now," I added. Hopefully she'd hurry along if only for the opportunity to share a few chosen words with me.

Chapter 39

I relayed Lexi's news and said to Petra, "Can I…"

Something fell in the front hall. Petra and I stared at each other. But only for a second. "Looters," she mouthed. She unzipped the fanny pack at her waist and took out a small pistol. The dark at the head of the stairs breathed, alive and waiting. There was no way out. We were trapped there. I scooted behind the counter that separated the kitchen from the living area and ducked down. Petra followed.

I eased open a drawer and reached in for a weapon. My hand searched among the utensils before closing around a large handle. I pulled out a carving knife. My heart was pounding against my ribs. I took long deep breaths and let them out slowly, trying to calm myself. We waited. The stairs creaked.

The squeak of a runner on hardwood – even above the storm I heard that. We weren't alone anymore. Silence. We waited some more and then the huge man from the night before appeared at the end of the counter. He pointed his gun at us. He smiled.

Petra didn't wait, didn't ask questions or give him a chance to explain. She shot him.

The force of the bullet pushed him backwards against the refrigerator. His expression changed, his jaw seeming to drop in surprise, even as blood spurted from his neck. The spurt changed to a fountain. Unhurriedly at first, he slid sideways, leaving a fan of blood on the stainless steel as he fell. The gun clattered on the floor and spun away from him. Petra stood. Reaching out with her foot, she pulled his gun towards her. She swung around to face me.

I was still crouched down on my heels, the knife clutched in front of me with both hands.

"Put the knife down, Sherri."

I mewed, a thin whine of protest. I didn't want to let go of it, needed to keep it for comfort. I stared past her at the man. Was he dead? I couldn't find the words to ask. I watched, expecting him to shake himself and rise again, like a zombie, to kill us.

"Sherri." Petra's voice was loud and commanding above the howl of the wind. "Put down the knife."

Vomit rose in my throat.

"Sherri."

Get a grip, that voice in my head admonished. I laid the knife on the floor but I didn't stop staring at him. *Just like Clay.* The thought echoed in my head over and over.

Petra put her gun back in its pouch. "Stand up."

I stood, but I never took my eyes off his body. How had he found me? It didn't matter. He was dead.

Petra stepped between me and the dead man. She took me by the shoulders and shook me hard. The towel I'd wrapped around my wet hair fell to the floor. "Are you going into shock?" she asked.

Was I? I shook my head once.

Her hands were still on my shoulders. "Then speak to me."

"Holy shit!" I tore my eyes away from the body to ask, "Are you all right?"

"Sure." A crooked smile. "No sweat for an old vet, and not the first dead man I've seen."

"But is he the first man you've killed?" Why did I want to know? Perhaps I wanted to tell her that it wasn't over, may never be over. Like me and the man I'd killed, she'd see him forever in her nightmares.

She swung around to study the dead man. Her body was ridged with concentration.

I focused my eyes on the wall above the fridge, happy to have someone else in charge and stand there like a mannequin, waiting to be moved around, put in position, and told what to do.

"Okay," she said. "This is what we're going to do." She turned back to face me. "Can you hold yourself together?"

"I think so."

"Well, you bloody well have to if you want to help your friend."

I nodded. "I can do it."

"Okay. You were not here when this guy snuck up the stairs. You had already left."

I nodded in agreement.

She picked up the knife and put it back in the drawer, slamming it brutally shut, and then she unzipped her pouch and handed me a set of keys. "Take the jeep."

"I was going to ask you if I could borrow it when this guy showed up."

She wasn't interested in chatting. "Hop up on the counter. We don't want your footprints in the blood."

I did as she said and then sat there like a dummy.

"Now tell me again where you're going."

She read the confusion on my face. "The street signs may be down or blowing so hard you won't be able to read them. You don't want to get lost so tell me where you're going so we can be sure you've got it right."

I went over the directions again. "Okay." She bent over and picked up the towel I had dropped. Walking to the end of the counter, she took a big step to avoid the worst of the splatter and to keep her body as far away from the body as possible. She motioned me to her. I slid off the counter and went to join her. "You go first," she said. "I want my footprints to cover yours."

"Where are you going?" Nothing was making sense to me.

"I'm going to follow you downstairs and call the police from my apartment."

"But…"

"I'm too distraught to call from here." A wry smile before she added, "And I want to step everywhere you do. Move."

I moved.

Chapter 40

Petra was right about the street signs. The ones that were left oscillated madly in the wind, impossible to read. I went over and over the directions in my head. *Please let me get it right.* My sense of direction was erratic and undependable at the best of times. The address Lexi had given me was out near Fort Zachary Taylor State Park, the southernmost point of the continental United States. A U.S. naval base was out there. Petra told me how to orient myself from the base. But first I had to get to the tip of the island.

The roads were empty of cars, moving or otherwise, and the houses were all eerily dark. A river of trash flowed down the street in front of me. A plastic urn tumbled out of a laneway. The urn sounded like an explosion when it hit the jeep. I swung wildly to the right and struck the curb. The jeep tilted dangerously.

A hundred yards more the street lights went out. I slowed. The headlights on the jeep scarcely penetrated the darkness. I leaned forward, afraid of what I couldn't see. Within a block I was stopped by a palm tree that had fallen across the road.

I reversed back to the intersection I'd just passed and hesitated, trying to decide if it would be better to detour to the right or the left. So many roads seemed to dead end or twist and turn on themselves in this place. The last thing I wanted to do was get lost. I took a chance on turning left.

This direction took me closer to the ocean. Although Key West seems perfectly flat, the land must be lower here, because I found myself plowing through water at least six inches deep. I wasn't at all sure the motor wouldn't flood out, but the battered jeep kept going like the soldier it was. I went down two blocks before I cut back to my right, glad to be on higher and drier roads. The traffic lights were out and the stop signs had blown away. Cross streets jumped out of the dark at me. Going through intersections without stopping I could only hope that everyone had evacuated or were hiding somewhere safe.

Where was I? I'd been counting the cross streets to tell me how far I'd driven. How accurate my block count was... well, at best it was an estimate.

The neighborhood changed. In any other town, this would be called the better section, where houses were a little farther apart, a little more private. The headlights picked out the number twenty-two set in a stone pillar. It was the number I was looking for, but was it the right street? I pulled into the drive of a two-storied cream house with full length turquoise shutters. Was it the home of Jon's girlfriend? I wasn't certain. I leaned forward and studied it through the windshield. I'd hate to break into the wrong house and be shot as a looter.

It looked like it had been patterned after a Disney castle, all turrets and steep roofs. A veranda ran along the front of the house, and beside the shiny black door a bright carriage light glowed. At least the electricity was still on here. I drove up the brick laneway and struggled to exit the jeep. I was still holding onto the door when a gust of wind caught it, slammed it shut, and shoved me backwards along the side of the jeep.

Flattened against the vehicle by the wind, I stood there and stared at the mansion, trying to figure out what to do next. Metal shutters, fitted tight over the windows, didn't allow any light to escape from inside. Shutters were a sensible precaution when you were going away for a month. Fortified like that, no one would need to come and check on the house. But then, perhaps some prudent homeowner had rolled them down just this morning before leaving. Shit, I had no way of knowing if this was the place I was looking for. If I was wrong, I just had to hope that McPhee would get it right.

The first thing I wanted to know was if there was a shed in the back yard. I'd been thinking about it so long and hard I'd convinced myself that was where I'd find Marley. I just had to walk up the driveway and into the backyard like I belonged there.

I slipped the sap from my pocket. Jon was likely working alone, but if there was someone guarding Marley I wanted to be ready. But even with the leaded weapon in my hand, I was no match for a man. Let's hope the metal shutters had blocked the jeep's headlights.

The bricked driveway along the right side of the house was lit by more black carriage lanterns on poles that wobbled in the wind. I walked slowly, fighting the wind.

Along the side of the house Confederate jasmine bloomed. Even in the storm I could smell the few flowers still clinging to the vines. At the black iron fence, that separated the driveway from the garden area, I pushed open the unlocked gate. Motion detectors came on. The first thing I saw was what wasn't there to be seen. There was no shed, no extra structures of any kind. But then rich people didn't need mundane things such as wheelbarrows and lawn mowers. Gardeners came to trim the palms in front of the plastered walls around the perimeter. More people came to clean the pool that took up most of the backyard, and the same workers probably swept the bricks that surrounded the pool, taking all their tools away with them. There was no need for a shed, which meant I hadn't found Marley.

The back garden would be a tropical paradise on a nice day. Tall palms grew in clumps around the solid wall, while climbing plants, bougainvillea, jasmine, and trumpet vine covered most of the white stucco. Right now, it was all in furious motion.

Red bricks stretched to the screened lanai along the back of the house. The screening had come loose and now flapped like a loose sail in the wind. There was no furniture on the lanai. Had it been taken inside ahead of Alma or did it mean that the owner was away? No way of knowing.

273

On the lanai, a wall of glass was covered by metal shutters. Beside the shutters, a French door was also protected by its own rigid barrier. The Yale lock was not something that could be opened by my small key.

I huddled against the house, arms crossed and my back to the wind, waiting for McPhee to show up. She didn't come. The lights went out. I waited some more. I really didn't want to go into the house alone. Lightning flashed and lit up the darkness, exposing deep shadows with hidden dangers. The palm fronds were giant hands reaching out for me.

I cursed. No more waiting. When I was a kid, besides bartending and working as a motel maid, my mom always had a housecleaning gig on Friday afternoons. When I was off school, and the owners weren't home, she took me with her. Here's a funny thing that I learned. Employers don't like to give the staff a key but they don't mind leaving one outside where the cleaner, or anyone else for that matter, can find it. I started to look. I searched above the door frame and under the mat of rubber flowers before I started moving out from the door and searching under the shrubs. The big rock was a dead giveaway. There are no rocks like that in Florida. I retrieved the key and opened the door.

I stepped inside.

Chapter 41

I hesitated. I couldn't hear any alarms. Nothing. A million-dollar home and I just walked in. Were silent alarms going off, bringing security guards? Would they come out in a hurricane to investigate or had they all left ahead of Alma? Looters were a big worry during an evacuation but alarms must be going off all over town and the chance of someone answering this one was just about nil.

I felt along the wall for a switch and turned on the light.

The overhead chandelier lit up an elegant room. More than that. The ground floor was one huge open space. Easy to see there was no one here.

Where do you look for a padlocked door? If you've kidnapped someone and need to hide them you'd want to keep them away from casual visitors. Going downstairs wasn't an option. In Florida, there are no basements. If you try to dig one, you'll have a swimming pool with a house on top. That left the upstairs and maybe an attic.

I crossed the room to the stairs. Dark floors had hidden what the white rug on the stairs quickly revealed: rust colored stains. Blood. Not a lot, but there were drops on the first three treads.

"Shit." I held my breath and listened hard. There was no human sound. Only the howling wind. "Hello," I yelled. I put my foot on the very edge of the first step, avoiding the blood. "Marley?"

I was sure I heard something. I paused and held my breath to hear better. Only half convinced it wasn't my imagination, I started up the stairs, slowly, climbing one step at a time, waiting on each stair to call out, "Hello." Halfway up I was sure I could hear something. It was coming from the right of the upper gallery. I ran. I stopped at the first door which was slightly ajar. I could hear muffled noises.

I pushed the door open on an unused and unloved guest bedroom. Marley wasn't there, but the pounding was louder.

There was another door. Unlike the bedroom, the bath had been remodeled. I could hear someone yelling for help and pounding on the wall. The noise seemed to come from inside the wallboard. I leaned against it and yelled, "Marley, it's Sherri." The noise stopped. And then there was a scream from inside the partition.

I ran out into the hall and along the corridor to the next room, a small den. At the back of the room, between ceiling high bookcases, was a door with a shiny-new clasp.

I dug out the key. "Just a minute," I yelled. My hands shook so much I couldn't connect the key and the lock. "It's all right," I babbled. "You're fine." I jammed the key into the lock. All the while she was shouting at me, neither of us listening to the other. With my disobedient hands, it seemed to take an enormous amount of time, but finally the lock was undone. I turned the knob and pushed hard. The door slammed back against the wall of a small powder room that had been carved out of the larger guest bath. There was a toilet and a sink, but no window.

Marley, trembling and barely upright, stood before me. Wearing only mauve underpants and a matching lace bra, her lips were bloodless, her green eyes huge with shock. "It's you. How..." And then she stumbled over to me and grabbed me, sobbing and saying over and over, "It's you."

"I told you it was me." She wasn't listening, hadn't taken it in and didn't care. She slumped against me, crying. I pulled her left arm over my shoulder and put my right arm around her waist. Half carrying her, but mostly dragging her, we made our way out into the hall.

Marley clutched at me. "Sherri?" I heard the question in her voice. She lifted her terrified and uncertain face to me.

I understood. Even when you are rescued, you don't quite believe it. Safety is a state of mind, not a reality. "It's okay," I said. "There's no one in the house." What made me so sure of that? I shivered at the thought.

We were nearly at the stairs when we heard a sound that said we were not alone. And then the lights went out.

Chapter 42

Marley and I clutched each other. The lights came back on. A voice shouted, "Police. Put down your weapons and show yourself."

Marley slumped against me. A dead weight, I couldn't hold her. She fell to her knees. I let her go and said, "It's okay. It's McPhee."

"Police. Show yourself immediately."

"It's Sherri Travis," I yelled. "I have Marley with me."

"Put your hands over your head and come to the head of the stairs."

I did as I was told. When I left the protection of the hall I saw her. Her drawn gun, supported by both hands, was pointed at me. That's when I remembered what Lexi had told me about the Key West police department being declared a criminal organization. Had I made a terrible mistake? I froze in place, watching and waiting. I saw McPhee's shoulders relax. She said, "Drop your weapon."

"What weapon?"

"The one you're holding."

Only then did I realize I still had the zap in my hand. I let it drop.

Slowly, McPhee lowered her gun, but she didn't holster it.

"Where's the other one?"

Anger. "Her name is Marley." She didn't even care enough to know Marley's name. "She's right here." I turned to help Marley to her feet.

"Stay where you are," McPhee shouted. The gun was pointed at me again.

"She can't walk on her own."

Hugging the wall, McPhee started up the stairs. Her arms were stretched straight out in front of her, the gun centered on my body. Step by deliberate step, she climbed the stairs.

When she was almost to the top she motioned with her head. "On the wall with your hands over your head."

"Jesus…"

"Do as I say." That voice left no room for doubt. She would shoot me if I didn't obey. I obeyed.

I heard her moving but I didn't risk even twitching to see what she was doing.

"Do you really think I have nothing better to do than chase all over Munro County for you?" she said.

For once I managed to keep my mouth shut.

"You can put your hands down."

I did and turned cautiously to face her. She still held the gun but it was no longer pointing at me. "She was locked in a bathroom." I gestured with my head. "Down there."

"You should have waited before you entered the house." McPhee's standard mood seemed to be pissed off, but I laughed anyway.

"If I'd waited for you, nothing would happen."

McPhee looked like she wanted to chew nails and spit tacks.

I risked moving, going to Marley and wrapping my arms around her. She fell back against me. "Marley's safe," I pointed out to McPhee, as if she hadn't noticed yet. "Everything's fine."

"Except you broke into this house."

"But I called you," I said, as if that made it legal.

"You broke in."

"There was no time for a court order. With the storm, how long would it take you to get a warrant?"

She grimaced.

"There's several millions of dollars of drugs hidden somewhere in this house," I told her. "I'm sure Jon brought it here when he hid Marley."

She looked from Marley to me and then she jabbed her forefinger at me and said, "Wait here." Gun held out in front of her, she went down the hall to check out Marley's prison.

McPhee called in reinforcements and started searching for the drugs. It didn't take long to find them. They were still in the pantry where Jon had hidden them.

Once help arrived, McPhee insisted that Marley go to the hospital and get checked out. Procedure, it seemed. Marley took some persuading. She just wanted to get in her car and leave Key West. She didn't care about the hurricane winds, the rain bucketing down, or giant waves covering the causeways, ready to wash us out to sea. Nothing mattered but getting away from her nightmare. She stood there, nearly naked and shivering, and used language on McPhee that I'd never heard come out of Marley's mouth before.

McPhee took it all in stride, stripping a blanket off a bed and wrapping it around Marley while gently soothing her. "I'll take her in my car," McPhee said.

I wasn't fooled. McPhee wasn't at all sure I wouldn't try to leave Key West if Marley was with me. I didn't waste my breath trying to convince her, just gave her my word that I'd follow meekly behind. But I had a stop to make first. Well, two stops.

A police car blocked the street in front of Petra's house. A hearse stood in front of the gate. I left the jeep running, afraid the wet engine wouldn't start again if I shut it off. The wind blew me sideways and at one point I crashed into the fence before fighting my way back onto the sidewalk.

There was no one posted at the door to stop me from entering. "Petra," I called.

She came out from the back of the house. "Are you all right?" I asked.

"I'm fine," she said. I nodded, agreeing to her lie. Her arms were wrapped tightly across her chest. Her face was pale, her vibrancy gone. Now she looked her age. Shooting someone does that to you.

"I found Marley. She's at the hospital."

She smiled.

"I'm going to pick up Lexi. Come with me."

She glanced up the stairs, then quickly back at me. She didn't ask permission, didn't tell the police working the crime scene upstairs where she was going. She went out the door ahead of me, too soon to see the stretcher bearers starting down the stairs with a body.

At the hospital, they wanted to do a rape kit. Apparently, Marley was taking some convincing.

The nurse coming out of Marley's room said, "That's some vocabulary your friend has."

"I don't know where she could possibly have learned it," I said, putting my hand on my chest in distress. "She comes from such a good family."

The nurse gave me a skeptical look. "See if you can talk her into an examination."

But Marley just wanted to go get her Neon and leave.

"It's too late," I said. "In case you didn't notice, there's a hurricane kicking the shit out of us. We can't get over the causeway. The hospital is the safest place to ride out the storm. Besides, the doctor wants you to stay. Do as you're told." I stretched out on the bed beside her. I was beyond tired.

"You'll ruin that clean bed," Lexi said. "You're soaking wet."

I groaned and rolled off the bed and collapsed on the uncomfortable guest chair.

Lexi said, "I'll find some towels," and headed for the door. At the door, she stopped. "Come with me, Petra." She waited with the door open. "You know where to find things in a hospital." Petra had told Lexi about shooting a looter in the upstairs kitchen and now Lexi was reluctant to let her out of her sight, sure Petra was suffering from post-traumatic stress.

"The cops need a statement," I told Marley when the door closed behind them. "You need to tell them what happened." I yawned. Exhaustion had replaced terror.

"I don't want to tell anyone what happened." She curled onto her side to face me. "I was a fool. Cheap and easy, it was my own fault."

"No, it wasn't. You went to see a show. That's all you agreed to. It was Jon's fault. He drugged you. You're the victim here."

Marley squirmed and pulled the hospital gown further up her neck. "I feel like a fool, believing that he fell for me the
283

moment he saw me." She picked at her gown. "I knew it wasn't true, knew there was something else going on, but I wanted to ignore it and go with the fantasy, the exciting vacation romance. I was stupid and now people are dead."

"You didn't kill them." I yawned again. "Let it go."

She lifted her head. "Can you hear yourself? Isn't that what I told you after Clay died?"

"Tell me what happened."

Drifting in and out of sleep, I listened to Marley's story. It was pretty simple. Jon wanted to take her for a moonlight drink on the beach. Marley's mojito came with knock-out drops. She'd woken up in the bathroom, stripped of her clothes and being violently sick. The water in the taps was shut off. She stayed alive by drinking out of the toilet tank.

I roused myself enough to ask, "How did your blood get in his vehicle?"

Marley held up her hand. There was a giant gash from the base of her thumb to the center of her palm. "I have no idea how it happened. I doubt he even knew it was there." She shrugged. "I don't remember anything from the time I drank that pretty little cocktail until I woke up on the bathroom floor."

I said, "There's something you should know."

Her eyes grew wide with apprehension.

"Jon is dead."

"Good!" The word exploded out of her. She rolled away. Rigid, and pulled into a tight ball, she sobbed.

284

I got up and sat on the edge of the bed to rub her shoulder. "Look, I know I've been driving you crazy, but don't give up on me, will you?"

She gave a little hiccup and looked up over her shoulder at me. "You mean like you gave up on me? McPhee told me all about it on the ride over." She snuffled into the coverlet and then she said, "Remember when Tully used to tell us, 'Come home together, or don't come home at all?'"

"Yup."

"I finally figured out what that meant. He was telling us to watch out for one another."

"He's a weird old bastard, isn't he?"

A burst of laughter and she then said, "I love your old man."

"And we do look out for one another, don't we?"

"Always have, always will." She reached up and patted my hand. "Face it; we're stuck with each other until the bitter end."

"Well, I can hack it if you can."

"I can," she mumbled.

I went back to the chair and was asleep within minutes. Apparently, the nurses tried to wake me, but Marley made such a fuss they let me sleep while they did the blood work and the rape test.

I woke with my heart racing from a dream of someone holding me by the foot and pulling down into water. Marley moaned, having her own bad dreams. The storm raged with a sound like a freight train coming toward us but never arriving. Lexi was sleeping on the floor by my chair. I pulled my foot out from under her. She rolled away but didn't wake. I lifted my head to look at Petra, sleeping in the chair Lexi had brought in from the waiting room for her. I put my head down again. The wind howled to get in, but we were out of danger. Best of all, I wasn't alone.

Strangely, lying there with the storm wailing outside, a powerful feeling of peace and joy came over me. My life hadn't contained a lot of those feelings. Safe, that's what I felt, and surrounded by a warm cocoon of love and friendship. While the outside world battered at the walls, for the first time since Clay's death I thought about my future and a life on my own. It was a subject I'd been avoiding but it no longer scared me.

Somewhere towards morning the freight train winds died down and calm came. The eye of the storm was passing over us. The second half of the storm was yet to come but for now we were fine. "Lexi," I whispered. She didn't answer. "Lex." I prodded her with my toe. With a grunt, and then a sigh, she turned stiffly over onto her back. Minutes passed. She cursed softly and sat up and began to stretch.

"I got an offer for you," I said.

She stretched and yawned. "If it's to change places, I'll take it. My back is killing me."

"How would you feel about being a partner in the Sunset?"

She jerked around to face me. "You're kidding."

"Nope."

"Fifty-fifty?"

"In the restaurant business only. Not the building."

She rubbed the small of her back as she thought about it. "Sounds good, but do you think Jac is ready for my return? I might hurt your business. It's a pretty Southern Baptist small-town."

"Hell, yeah! We've been waiting for you."

Late in the afternoon, the remnants of Alma had dissipated. The sun shone brilliantly and the nurses had no more sympathy for us, so we piled into Petra's sodden jeep and headed out to check on the town. About four inches of water still covered the roads, and we had to make two detours because of debris and trees, but Key West was still there.

Petra wanted to see her home and, as she'd predicted, it had survived just fine. One piece of yellow police tape still fluttered from the top of the front door. A second piece was tangled in the oak tree, a sight that for no good reason sent us all into gales of laughter. McPhee had told us Lexi's apartment was still a crime scene so we weren't allowed to go in. None of us wanted to be there anyway. We went to the Rawhide. There was a bit of damage, shingles missing, a broken window and vegetation strewn about, but the electricity was on, so we had food and water and plenty of booze. We moved in.

We began the cleanup by sweeping off the porch and taking out the rocking chairs. By dinnertime, Marley was sitting out on the porch with a beer in her hand and her feet up on the railing. I dropped into a rocker beside her. "How are you feeling about Lexi coming to Jacaranda?"

"Good." A change had taken place in Marley. She was no longer the person who had left the Rawhide arm in arm with Elvis. She tipped the neck of the bottle toward me in a salute. "I'm just hoping you'll introduce Lex to Bernice and all her lovely friends with their wide butts and narrow minds." The impish smile was back on her face. "Maybe they'll all choke on the olives in their martinis."

"Now, that's something to look forward to."

Silence stretched between us. At last I said, "Don't become bitter."

"You mean like you?"

I thought about it. Was I bitter? More like disillusioned and shell-shocked.

Marley said, "Friends, we need friends to watch our back. I'm glad Lexi is coming home."

Two days later we had McPhee's permission to leave. Tanya's input helped. In fact, it was Tanya who went with us to pick up our clothes. We weren't allowed in the apartment alone.

Packing didn't take long. Marley and I were both determined to get out of there fast. This time, heading back across the Everglades, Marley drove while I put my feet up on the dash and sang along with the radio.

We didn't talk about the past. For once we only talked about the future. A fantasy future perhaps. It didn't really matter. The fun was in the planning.

Phyllis Smallman's first novel, **Margarita Nights**, won the inaugural **Unhanged Arthur** award from the Crime Writers of Canada. Her writing has appeared in both **Spinetingler Magazine** and **Omni Mystery Magazine**. Her Sherri Travis mystery series was chosen by **Good Morning America** for a summer read in 2010. The Singer Brown series won the **gold medal** from **Independent Publishers**.
Before turning to a life of crime, Smallman was a potter.

Visit her at www.phyllissmallman.com

If you enjoyed this book, please consider writing a review on Amazon, Kobo, Good Reads, Facebook or the platform of your choice. It doesn't have to be much more than, "I liked this book." Reviews get a reader's attention and help authors sell books.

Made in the USA
Lexington, KY
24 March 2018